The Raided Heart

Jennifer C. Wilson

ISBN: 9781695418035

Cover image: SarahRichterArts via Pixabay
Cover design: Jennifer C. Wilson
Editor: Sue Barnard

First published 2019 by Jennifer C. Wilson and Ocelot Press

DEDICATION

To the spirits of Carnasserie Castle, where all my historical fiction adventures began.

CONTENTS

ACKNOWLEDGEMENTS

The Raided Heart has been a long time in the making…

I've referred to it as the "Trigger's Broom" of stories – it's had multiple rewrites, changing setting, time period, and a couple of sub-plot changes, but throughout, the same core plotline has managed to survive for over twenty years now. A huge thanks to everyone who has listened to me talk about this at any point in the last two decades then, but more recently, thanks to members of Elementary Writers for providing feedback on sections of the work-in-progress, and to Penny Blackburn, Alex Heppell, Jane Roberts-Morpeth and Sarah Jeffery for their encouragement, and simply not letting me give up on it, even when I declared I was giving up writing for good!

I'm also grateful to Sue Barnard for her excellent editing support, as always, helping me polish the manuscript, as well as advising on some key plot changes which had, if I'm honest, been bothering me during this rewrite.

Final thanks, as always, go to my parents, for again, the encouragement to keep going, especially as it got so close to the final version, and for taking me to Carnasserie Castle, where inspiration first hit, all those years ago.

CAST OF CHARACTERS / KEY DEFINITIONS

At Long Ridge

Meg Mathers
Robert Mathers
Judd Mathers
Will Hetherington
Hannah Carstairs
Ben Fraser
Lizzie Wilkinson
Cecily Reed
Tom Reed

At Cliffside

Alexander Gray
Bridget Gray
Henry Gray
Hal Robson
John Robson
Claire Wilson
Sarah Martin
Katherine (surname unknown)

Others

Richard, Duke of Gloucester (younger brother of King Edward IV), and Warden of the West March
Jarvis, Deputy Warden of the Middle March
The Elliots

Key Definitions

Bastle: A fortified farmhouse, common along the English-Scottish border, designed to protect the residents against raiders.
Reiver: Raiders along both sides of the English-Scottish border, prevalent between the 13th and 17th centuries.
Hot trod: A counter-raid, legally mounted, within six days of a family or village falling foul of a raid.
Cold trod: A counter-raid, as above, but after six days, and requiring approval in law.

CHAPTER ONE

Long Ridge, Northumberland, October 1471

The dark still wasn't moving.

Meg Mathers stood at the window of the family's bastle, trying to pick out any hint of movement, friend or foe, against the blue-black of the night, but there was none to be found. It had been hours since the men had ridden out – it couldn't be much longer now. Without looking down, she polished the pewter dish in her hand once again; she didn't know how many times she had cleaned it already that night, but she couldn't stop. Just as she knew that behind her, Hannah Carstairs and Lizzie Wilkinson would be equally lost in equally meaningless repetition.

Behind each dot of light in the cottages beyond the enclosure's defensive wall, it would be the same. The women, the old, the young and the infirm, each finding their own way to pass the hours until fathers, husbands, brothers and sons were safely returned to them. None were aware of what they were doing; the cloth in Meg's hand could rub away to nothing and the fact wouldn't have registered. At least it felt productive.

As much as Meg hated seeing them go on each raid, it was a necessity this time. One more failed try, and the dreaded possibility of over-winter starvation might just become their reality. Meat was already running low.

She kept staring into the dark.

***

"Come on lad, we can make it!" Robert Mathers yelled at the top of his voice.

Will Hetherington was uncertain whether his leader was encouraging his horse, himself, or Will. It didn't really matter; either way, they needed to speed up. In the muddle of hooves, equine and bovine, Will was no longer sure whether the horses he could hear were just from their own gang, or if they were being pursued by their victims. Seven fat cattle were certainly a prize worth chasing after, if the farm had noticed their theft.

He wanted to stop, to allow Robert to take stock, to check the hilltops which surrounded them for beacons, or the tiny dots of flaming peat cuts (the sure sign they were being pursued), to check whether they might be heading into a trap, but there was no time. Long Ridge was still miles away by his reckoning, and only then if they stayed on the right path – easier said than done in the race to safety from a raid, in the dead of night, and with just a hint of fear constantly at the back of your mind. He trusted the two brothers leading them, but mistakes could still happen. He was far too aware of that.

Will blinked away the memories which threatened to return. He had to focus, this was no time to wallow.

***

At Long Ridge, the three women had moved on from cleaning to pretending to sew, tackling the mound of torn shirts and worn jackets their assorted menfolk had thrust at them during the previous days. A pointless activity, with the candles providing only a fraction of the light they needed, and leading to plenty of mistakes which would no doubt need fixing when the valued daylight returned. They huddled around the window now, needles frozen in their hands.

More dim candlelight had appeared in the windows of the nearby cottages too now, leaving only Hannah's and Lizzie's in darkness, as the rest of the community waited – either for their own menfolk to return, or for the sign they needed to retreat to the safety of the tall, towering bastle house, draw up the ladders and stairways, and hope they could withstand whatever onslaught befell them. Even within the thick, solid walls, it wasn't guaranteed.

Meg tore her eyes away from the window for a moment to check the fire was still blazing, with the jugs of wine and ale warming nearby for when they were needed.

It couldn't be long now.

***

"A light!"

The cheer made its way down the path, from Judd Mathers, at the head of the group now, past Robert, finally reaching Will and his friend Ben Fraser as they brought up the rear. Will pushed his horse on, spurring forward to join the two brothers, their leaders.

"Long Ridge?" he asked, hoping.

"Aye laddie, I recognise the pattern," replied Judd, grinning. "We've made it, my friend."

"I'll not relax until this lot is in the enclosure," Robert replied, with the sense of an established leader, and pulling on Champion's reins to check everyone made it down the final steep descent before the incline back to their village. Even so close to home, nobody could relax. Mistakes were most easily made when you thought you were already safe.

***

Horses. No mistaking it. At least twenty, although the darkness made counting impossible. But the shadows heading along the path to the village definitely included horses, and, to Meg's relief, the slow steady pace of cattle in amongst them. If they could defend their prize, they could make the winter. They would be safe. If. But worrying on that wouldn't help now. Meg, Hannah and Lizzie pulled up the trapdoor and descended two floors to the ground floor store-room, dragging open the great wooden doors just as the men reached the gate of the stone enclosure which surrounded their bastle, giving an extra layer of defence when needed.

She watched as her brothers opened the tall gate, and led in their horses, before beckoning the others to follow. There was chaos now, as women flooded in from the cottages to welcome home their menfolk. Meg counted as best she could, with nobody staying still longer than a heartbeat; they didn't seem to have lost anyone. It was a relief. She smiled to herself as she began her usual task, checking the precious horses back into the lower floor of the bastle. The cattle would be safe enough in their fortified barn beyond the wall, but they had to be doubly careful with their steeds. The men filed in, as caring for their horses as they had ever been, or ever would be, for wives and children, passing the reins to Meg as they greeted her warmly, as the matriarch of the village she had become, on her mother's death.

***

Will was the last through the huge door. Not having been at Long Ridge that long, he was still finding his feet amongst the camaraderie of his fellow-riders, although they had acknowledged he was a good raider, despite his young age and lack of real blood-link to the village. His sister Cecily had vouched for him, having been married to a local lad, Tom Reed, for the past five years, and gained the Mathers' trust. Now he brought in his beloved mare, fussing over her as she grew fractious at the noise around her, in such a small space. Keeping one hand rubbing her ear, he threw the reins over the nearest spare beam. He preferred to do this himself, rather than letting Meg do it; however good Meg seemed to be with the animals, Patience was his horse, and he knew how best to care for her.

He hadn't noticed the lady of the house approaching with another horse, seeking to tie this one up beside Patience. Hadn't sensed her momentary distraction as she threw the reins over the beam beside him. Hadn't noticed Patience's hint of fear as the reins glanced her ear, spooking her. The sudden rush of fear caused her to rear up, constrained and frightened in the enclosed area, even more so as Will had already fastened her reins tightly to stop her straying. She thrashed about, with everyone rushing to calm her.

Then, suddenly, she side-stepped into Meg.

***

At first, Meg didn't notice the pain.

Then it began to spread: a warm sensation, rushing through her foot and ankle over the next few heartbeats, and now a strange feeling growing up the lower half of her leg. She ignored it; it was nothing but a strange reaction to the relief of the group making it home safely. A new reaction, true, but things could change over the years, she told herself.

Only when the movement around her slowed for a moment did she realise she wasn't able to put her foot wholly on the floor, with pain shooting through her whole body. Unable to stop herself, she cried out loud and grabbed at the nearby doorframe to keep herself upright, as Robert and the young raider rushed to her side, albeit with very different expressions on their faces.

"It's nothing! It's nothing!" Meg cried, hoping neither would make a fuss over her. She just needed to get to her bed, to rest. She couldn't afford to be injured. She could work through the pain.

It was too late, as her brother took charge, turning on the young lad at his side. "Will, what the hell do you think you're playing at, letting your animal knock her flying? If this is broken…"

"I didn't 'let' my animal do anything, Sir – she was spooked, that's all, by the reins going over the beam." Will spoke back, probably more strongly than he intended.

"So it's Meg's fault, is that what you're saying?" Robert snapped back. "No other horse has ever sent her flying."

"Gentlemen, please, I was not sent flying anywhere. I'm fine." Meg tried to argue, but Robert was having none of it, insisting that Will apologise for something he evidently didn't even see as his fault.

Even so, the young man made an attempt to put things right, already shrugging off his jacket and wrapping it clumsily around Meg's foot. "Is it broken?"

Meg could see that even as he asked about her ankle, one eye was on Patience. The mare was being calmed by Judd, who had shooed the other men out of the way.

"I can't tell. I don't think so. Probably just a sprain," replied Meg between gasps through her teeth. She hoped she was right; a broken ankle was the last thing any of them needed at the start of the winter.

Without allowing her another word of complaint, Robert had hoisted her into his arms, and carried her up to her bed. Unable to stand the growing pain any further, Meg slumped against him, heartbroken that in that moment, she didn't have the strength to fight the faint she knew was coming..

CHAPTER TWO

A combination of pain and sunlight woke Meg the next morning, as her mind was flooded with the memory of the late night, the hustle, the bustle, and the weight against her ankle. That, and Will. That stupid lad who had let his horse put her out of action for goodness knows how long, if the pain in her lower leg was anything to go by. He had only appeared in the village a short while ago, she knew that much about him, but hardly anything more, other than that her brothers had been impressed with his skill and courage on a raid, and the quality of his horsemanship. Heading over the border in raids was not a role for the faint of heart, and her brothers only let the best of men join them, especially on the riskier raids. One false move, and it wasn't just a loss of meat they would have to worry about: capture could well finish up at the end of a rope. She shook her head to clear the horrible image.

In the course of the various raids Will had been part of, or the events Long Ridge celebrated together over recent months, she had seen him around the village, and her own home, but he hadn't exactly stood out. She wasn't even entirely sure why he had moved there, or where his family was from, other than his sister Cecily being part of their community. She smiled as she thought back to how tenderly he had treated her the night before, despite his obvious anger at the situation. She suspected he would much rather have been tending to his horse than her. Still, he had been better than some of the men of Long Ridge, and their tendency towards the brutish – even her beloved brothers. Yes, Robert and Judd loved her dearly, she was confident in that, but they would never dream of showing it. Or if they did, it would be through the provision of the finest wine, or capturing the fattest cattle they could find for her. In their world, meat mattered.

Will, despite his bitterness, had been different: gentle,

with both her and his horse, before it had trampled her ankle. She found herself wondering what he was up to at that very moment, over in the small cottage he shared with his sister and her husband. She didn't have long to wait to find out. A heartbeat later, she heard the heavy trapdoor from the bastle's lower level being thrown open a floor below her, and men's voices fill the silence.

"You'll take responsibility for your actions, lad! You got her into this mess, you can take care of her until she's out of it!" Robert was shouting, as heavy-booted footsteps kept coming, up another level and into the siblings' private living space. Well, as private as it got, with the three of them.

Meg scrambled with the bedclothes, making sure she was decently covered, just as Robert pulled back the curtain which separated her bed from the rest of the room. Will was half a step behind him, head bowed, face flushed, his dark brown hair mussed, giving the impression of a man who had suffered a bad night's sleep, and been rudely awoken without warning. Meg suspected she knew who the guilty party was in that regard.

"What use is she, out of action – for what, six weeks, two months – until she can put weight on that ankle again?" demanded Robert of the younger man. "You know how important she is to us all, to the village."

"I did apologise. It was an accident." The anger in Will's voice was clear, even as he tried to hide it.

Robert's face softened slightly, for a moment, then the hardness returned. "I know it was, lad; we all know nobody in Long Ridge would harm Meg deliberately. But still, she's in no fit state to tend to anything in the coming weeks. How is it?" He turned to her at last.

"Sore. Very sore," Meg confessed, to her shame. "And I couldn't put any weight on it earlier, when I tried to get up in the night."

"See," said Robert. "Anyway, the lad's going to be taking care of things, and you, until you're more mobile."

Both parties looked to Robert with a jolt.

"Will? No, but, surely Hannah would be a better choice?"

"And Sir, I have my own duties. I cannot be a lady's maid for, as you say, six weeks, or even two months!"

Robert silenced them both with a raised hand. "Hannah will be around, as always, I'm sure, but Will got you into this state, and he can sort things out too. Think of what you do around here, what with sorting the animals, looking after us when we get back, keeping this place in order. You'll never manage all of that, and it's not fair on Hannah to expect her to pick up everything."

Robert's logic was unfailing, and Meg knew he was right. Second to her, Hannah was the closest thing Long Ridge's bastle had to having a mistress of the house, as well as being Judd's long-standing (and long-suffering) mistress.

"I'll do everything I can, Robert, Sir, you know I will, and to the best of my abilities," said Will, glancing at Meg with narrowed eyes.

She blinked at him, unsure, but certain there had been malice in that look.

"I'm sure your best will be quite good enough, William," she found herself replying. She wasn't sure where 'William' had come from, apart from an odd need to somehow formalise this odd relationship they were being forced into for the foreseeable future. She had a feeling it wasn't going to be a comfortable time.

Robert had turned back to Will again. "So, we're resolved. I don't want you leaving her side, as long as decency permits, you hear me?"

The younger man nodded, his face dark. Meg suspected he was trying not to scowl, as Judd joined them in the chamber, fastening the belt of his sword at his hip. Immediately, Robert was alert, his mind clearly concerned with higher matters.

"Trouble?"

"What? No? Oh, this," said Judd, indicating his sword. "No, just thought I'd give the young lads something to do this morning, whilst the rest of the village recover from last night's raid: watch out in case of retribution. Keeps them out the way for a while too. If you're happy with that? Not as though you can keep them busy with your stories this morning, eh pet?" Without waiting to be asked, he sat himself down at the edge of Meg's bed, and with the easy disrespect of an elder sibling threw back the bottom of the blanket to check on her ankle.

"Judd! We have company," Meg objected, trying and failing to pull her ankle from his solid grip.

"Company that won't argue with me," said Judd, inspecting the damage. It was true. The oldest of the men present, he may have been only a half-brother to her and Robert, but content to let his legitimate younger sibling take charge following the death of their father. Relationships between legitimate and illegitimate siblings were not always so easy, and Judd never did anything to harm theirs. He manipulated her foot, paying no heed to her complaints regarding pain or decency. "Not broken, I reckon, just badly twisted and bruised. You'll live." He winked at her, gaining a swipe at the back of his head as a reward.

"Just go and send Hannah up here, would you? I'm in need of some female assistance."

"What makes you think I'd know where Hannah is?" Judd grinned.

Meg sighed. As usual, Judd was not willing to fully admit, even to his own family, the true commitment of his relationship with Hannah.

"If that's your attitude, it's just as well I always know where you are then, isn't it, Judd Mathers?" Nobody had noticed the lady in question arrive, bustling in carrying a dish of water and a drying sheet. Hannah Carstairs always knew how to handle a situation; that much could never be disputed. "Come on, out with you all. I'll give poor Meg a hand, and then you can come back in and see what's what."

The men left without question, only Judd hanging back to greet Hannah with a brief kiss.

"Away with you, man; go give those youngsters something to do." She turned to Meg. "Now, let's get you ready for the day."

CHAPTER THREE

An hour later, Hannah let the three men back into Meg's part of the chamber, drawing back the thick woollen curtain and appraising them with a raised eyebrow.

"She's fine, but that ankle means no weight on it at all for a good couple of weeks I reckon, and rest for another couple of months after that. It needs to be rested properly, well, as best you can in a place like this." She pointed at Will. "You'll be doing all the heavy lifting she would otherwise have been doing, and bring her downstairs every day. There's plenty she can be doing sitting at the table which will still be useful for us all. But I'll want you on hand just in case we need anything."

"I'm not an invalid, and I'm certainly not deaf," Meg called from her position, perched at the edge of her bed. She was now clad in a warm dress of blue wool, with her thick red-brown hair tied into a rough bun at the nape of her neck to make it easier for her to be carried. She could tell that the usual long, untied hair of an unmarried woman was not going to be practical for the next couple of weeks.

Hannah tutted, and nodded to Will to fetch Meg. He moved over to the lady who would be the centre of his world for the coming weeks, then paused, as though unsure of his next move.

Meg looked up at him, feeling as awkward as she was sure he did in that moment. Not wanting to stand on ceremony, she reached up and put an arm around his neck, and he bent to slide his arm beneath her legs. Luckily, he was a strong and competent young man, and in one easy movement, she was cradled in his arms, held close so there was no risk of him either falling, or dropping her. She knew that would not go down well with either of her brothers. Without meeting the eyes of anyone, especially not Will, Meg hung on as tightly as she could as he made his way across the room and down the short flight of stairs to the middle level of the bastle. Happily, for Meg, he didn't make an issue of things, and soon had her safely installed in the seat by the fire.

"Are you alright there?" he asked, stiltedly, his eyes already on the door.

"Better now I feel more refreshed," Meg answered him honestly. It was true; getting into a clean gown, having spent the night sleeping in the one she had worn for the whole of the previous day, had made her feel much more comfortable.

Robert had followed them down the stairs and was now sitting on the small dais at the far end of the room, at the table which was currently being used as a writing desk. Writing wasn't his greatest strength, but he took pride in it when he had to do it. He was focusing on the sheet of paper in front of him, as though playing through the words in his head before committing them to ink.

"What is it, Robert?" Meg called to him from her place at the fire, as Will brought a tray laden with bread and cheese to break her fast. "Anything I can help with?"

"The Wardens will be passing through our village in a couple of weeks, ahead of the Day of Truce; I intend to ask them to dine with us. Given Gray's recent activity, I want them to know that we are disapproving, and are, of course, always the Wardens' true allies in any disputes which might arise."

"The men of Cliffside? The men you ran into last week? The men you offered sanctuary to, here, in our home? And you say you are the Wardens' ally in any disputes?" Meg raised an eyebrow at her brother. She knew that at times the politics of their region offered little in the way of logic, but this was a step further than her brother usually went. Alexander Gray's local reputation for brutality, even for a reiver, was well known.

"I see no reason why we should give the Wardens any cause to doubt us, not with winter just around the corner, and our barn still not quite as full as it could be. We need to be careful, little sister. I may not condone carrying two flags just yet, but we may as well play both sides of our own border, don't you think?"

Meg wished she could jump up, lean at him across the table and look at him straight in the eye. Instead, she shifted as best she could in her seat, and fixed him with a level stare.

"Do you intend to work with Cliffside? From what I hear, Alexander Gray is a hard man."

"You hear right. Which is why, surely, it is better to be with him, rather than risk being against him. He has escaped the noose three times already, through his cunning. I would take any opportunity to work with him with caution, but I would still take it."

She was about to respond, but at that moment Ben, one of the most reliable younger men of the village, appeared at the top of the staircase.

"Robert, there's trouble over in the barn. Seems one of our new herd got a little adventurous in the night, managed to break down one of the stalls, and broke its own leg in the process. Would you come and take a look and see if we can keep her alive, or whether she'd be best slaughtered now? We'll get on with fixing the stall."

Sighing, Robert rose from the table. He collected the paper, pen and ink, carrying them over to Meg. "See what you can do, based on what I've started. You're better at this than me."

Meg smiled up at him, glad of a task she knew she could excel in, even when confined to a chair. After all, she had been writing letters on her brothers' behalf for as long as she could remember, and consistency was always crucial in such missives. Putting aside her food, she took up his work so far, resting it on the tray to see what she could add of use. If she had her way, the men of Long Ridge would have nothing to do with those of Cliffside.

CHAPTER FOUR

Despite the pain shooting up her leg at irregular intervals, Meg did her best to keep on with as much as possible of her administrative workload at the bastle. Sitting at her usual place at the table, she was running through the household accounts, checking Robert's calculations. She grimaced as a payment to one of their more powerful neighbours caught her attention.

"Not another payment to the Elliots!" she exclaimed.

"He didn't want to, but he had no choice." Judd's voice made her jump. Meg had assumed she was alone, apart from Will, who had taken to hovering at the far end of whichever space she was currently occupying, head bowed over his own work. Today, he was polishing Patience's bridle to within an inch of its life.

"There is always a choice. Why should we fall foul of this ridiculous blackmail, paying for their so-called 'protection' time after time?"

"Come on, lass, you didn't see the mess that Fourtracks was left in last summer."

Meg lowered her head. She might not have been there, but she had certainly heard the tales of bloodshed, kidnapping and theft. She had seen enough of the aftermath too, as distant kin of the Long Ridge villagers had made their way over the hills to their homestead. The injuries some had sustained didn't bear thinking of.

"We're not always strong enough on our own. A raid like our most recent, that pushes us far enough. Without the Elliots behind us, we might not always get away with it, or be able to pull off something greater, when it comes to it. You might not always have positive numbers in your accounts, or cattle in the barn." Judd pulled a chair out and sat beside her. "It's the way of the world, Meg. You know that; you've always known that. You're just angry it happened without you knowing about it, so you didn't have the chance to argue with your brother."

She scowled at him, but knew he was right. She glanced out of the window, and had the usual, odd feeling that the scenery was somehow mocking her. So beautiful, even in the middle of a snowstorm, and yet always hiding some hazard, some danger, whether human or natural. Instinctively, she pulled her shawl tighter around her.

"Fourtracks didn't pay then?"

Judd shook his head, drinking deeply from the mug of wine in front of Meg, and receiving a slapped hand for his troubles. "But we have. So we'll be alright."

"And what of Cliffside?"

"Cliffside?"

"Don't play innocent. I know Robert is looking to partner with Alexander Gray and his men. How does that fit in with the Elliots and their plan?" She picked up the mug herself, and took a sip.

"Has Cliffside ever been attacked by the Elliots, or been forced to pay their demands?" Will moved towards them, joining their conversation.

"No," Judd replied. "Gray's strong enough on his own. He has double our number – triple sometimes, when the nearby hamlets join him. He doesn't need the Elliots, and doesn't want to get involved."

"Then surely, if we partner with Cliffside, in any manner, we put ourselves at risk of conflict with the Elliots?" Meg could see Will's line of thought, and the thought of bringing the fate of Fourtracks down on Long Ridge was something which terrified her.

Judd didn't respond immediately, contemplating the ring on his middle finger. "We will tread a fine line."

"Too fine a line," countered Meg. "We're telling the Wardens that we are friendly with them, and that we monitor Cliffside and the Grays, whilst at the same time Robert is writing to Alexander, telling him that we won't betray him to the Wardens. And then, then, we still pay protection money to the Elliots. There are too many lines, all too fine for my liking."

"Meg, come on, you know how it is. We're some of the lucky ones, keeping our heads down. Don't give Robert a harder time than he gives himself. The Scots are particularly restless this year, nobody knows why. There's been violence almost every week. The taverns in Hexham and Carlisle are full of tales of hardship and terror. Frankly, whatever we can do to protect ourselves from that, I vote we do it."

"You've been all the way to Carlisle? Recently? Did you see the new Warden?" she asked. Everyone had heard of King Edward's brother being sent north to deal with the Scots.

"Gloucester?" Judd replied. "Aye, we saw him. Nothing but a lad, if you ask me, but he seems to be doing a good enough job. We can but wait and see."

Meg scowled again, returning to the accounts. From under her hair, she risked a glance at Will. He was looking over Judd's shoulder at a map, intent on studying the detail. Their enforced proximity this last week had certainly been a challenge, and she still didn't feel she knew him any better. Although, given his sullen attitude to her at times, she still wasn't sure she wanted to. Checking the prices they had paid for various items at market the previous week, she decided she should put such thoughts out of her mind. It was his fault she was in this situation, and the sooner it was over, the better.

CHAPTER FIVE

From his place across the top table from her at the communal evening meal that night, Will watched Meg observing the rest of the room. Hardly anything happened at Long Ridge without Meg knowing about it, and he was starting to see why. Her eyes were never still, and, he suspected, if her ears could flick between conversations as easily, they would. As it was, when she wasn't incapacitated by her ankle, she was always moving from group to group, when they had their weekly feasts in the main hall of the bastle. Today, he found himself sharing the honour of a place at the family's own table, ready to be summoned by a nod or a wave, should she need him. He hated being at her beck and call, just waiting for the next instruction. If she hadn't moved that wretched horse, they wouldn't be in this mess now – and, he suspected, both would be a lot happier too.

It was indeed a chore, being nothing but the servant of a young, headstrong girl like Meg, but he was starting to grudgingly admit that as he was spending more time with her, he could see why her brothers were some of the few men in the borders who took the advice of a woman seriously. She had a mature head on her shoulders, and one which was full of great ideas, along with the confidence to share them. Tonight, though, she was watching the younger members of the village, as they had pushed the table where they had been sitting back against the wall, making space for an impromptu dance to the music which two of the older men, sitting at another table across the room, had started playing. The mood over the meal had been sombre, as talk of raids had once again dominated the conversation. But now, with even Robert smiling, his foot tapping in gentle rhythm, the youngsters began to relax, evidently hoping the older members of the community would join them. Usually, Will would be there, showing off his fine dancing skills, but tonight, he had to be near Meg, and he found himself not bemoaning the fact.

A touch on his arm brought him back from his thoughts.

"My Lady, I'm sorry, I wasn't in the room." He forced politeness into his voice, trying to hide his resentment.

"I could see that. Where were you?" Meg smiled as she asked him, to show she wasn't worried that he hadn't been immediately paying her attention.

"My parents' kitchen, learning to dance with my sister. My mother always said that learning to dance would put me in good stead. For what, I'm not entirely sure, but perhaps being light on my feet has made me a half-decent raider?" His honest answer to her question surprised Will; he certainly hadn't intended to start sharing his past with the woman who was currently commanding his life.

"Able to follow a beat, move swiftly out of danger?"

"That's always the goal," he replied, smiling. Suddenly, the ale pushed its way to his head, making him reckless. "Perhaps one day, when you're back on your feet, we can share a dance?" The words had left his mouth before he fully realised what he was saying, but it was too late to take it back. He watched her face, trying to read her response before it was vocalised.

Meg's eyes narrowed as she focused on him, then brightened as a smile spread across her face. "I think that might just be allowed, William, if you do a decent job these next few weeks."

"I… I didn't mean to be so forward." Or so stupid, he berated himself. No matter, she would surely forget what he had said in a few moments, as the conversation moved on. He wouldn't make such a mistake again. It was the hair, he told himself; he had always had a soft spot for a redhead. Too late, he realised Meg was speaking again.

"Forward can be allowed, at times. Besides, you're a handsome young man, so what girl would I be to refuse you? Although, I might risk the wrath of others." She glanced across at a table of young women. Will followed her gaze, catching the eye of one or two he had indeed shared a dance with at previous village celebrations. He felt the heat rise in his cheeks.

Neither spoke for a while. Will pondered whether he even wanted to raise another topic for conversation with this curious woman. She was causing him plenty of trouble already, without adding communication into the mix. Since the accident, he had hardly ridden out on Patience, leaving her daily exercise to others, which irked him. But still, he truly had never met anyone like Meg; only his sister came close to being her equal in terms of wit and intelligence. Even now, he could tell she was half-listening to the talk between her brothers. The current topic was the quality of the meat from the deer they had managed to stalk and kill, but as soon as it moved onto more important subjects, such as the next raid, or the Warden's view of the next Day of Truce, he knew she would be involved in a heartbeat, finding out what was happening and making sure her opinion was taken into account.

He shuddered at the thought of the Day of Truce. An ancient borders rite, bringing representatives from England and Scotland together, it was ostensibly a day for criminals to be brought to be justice. That is, if their respective Wardens could track them down. More often than not, hardly any of the accused were found, and the day descended into chaos. That was what had happened two years ago this month, he thought, his mind threatening to wander again. Shaking his head, he pulled himself back into the present, to find Meg staring at him, a quizzical look on her face.

"You went away again," she said. "I'm going to have to keep an eye on you, if you keep wandering."

"My apologies. It won't happen again." He had to focus. The more his mind drifted back to that day, the more his history threatened to overwhelm him. He had found a home here at Long Ridge, and currently had a place amongst its leading family. He couldn't let that go.

"This won't be forever," Meg continued, a hint of relief in her voice. "I'll heal, and you can get back to your carefree days between raids."

"No, you misunderstand. I'm sorry. It isn't this." He gestured around them. "It's more, when I let it, my mind takes itself off to places I'm not keen on. Having you to focus on gives it less of a chance for that." Honesty, again. This had to be monitored.

She smiled. "Well then, perhaps my ankle will take a little longer than necessary to be fixed."

Her hand was once again on his arm, in comfort this time, rather than trying to attract his attention. With another brave moment pushing him onward, for a moment, he placed his on top of hers, and returned her smile.

CHAPTER SIX

The next morning felt different when Will came to collect Meg from her bed. There was still that hint of a begrudging nature from him, but she did feel as though she knew him fractionally more than she had the day before. He was not just another young hot-headed raider, trying to become the next hero of the borders, whose actions would be captured in one of their evening ballads, sung to while away the long cold dark winter nights. There was more to him than that. Something that gave him a mature seriousness that intrigued her, despite her frustration that he had been telling the others that she was to blame for the whole scenario. Meg couldn't remember the last time one of the young men of the village had intrigued her like this. Yes, there had been fleeting flashes of romantic thought when one of the good-looking lads had brought her a gift during the festive season, or held her closer than absolutely necessary when they danced at a village celebration, but they had been just that: fleeting.

Will certainly didn't make her heart leap when he walked into a room, but despite herself, and her crossness, she was starting to feel her spirits rise when she recognised his tread coming up the steps to the upper chambers. Just as she did now.

"Good morning, my lady," he greeted her, with a deep bow, but still a hint of mockery on his face.

"Good morning, kind sir," she returned in the same spirit, pulling herself to her feet as best she could. The pain in her foot was less severe after a week, but she still couldn't put her weight on it. She would be needing Will around for a good few weeks yet.

Arriving at the table, they found themselves alone; a note lay next to the food left out for Meg to break her fast.

"Gone to check the perimeters. Problems overnight at Fourtracks. Want to make sure we're visible today, in case anyone is still about. Have taken half the men. Stay indoors." Meg read aloud from the parchment, written in Robert's rushed hand. "Trouble in Fourtracks? What do you know?"

Will shook his head. "Only what's in the note. Cecily's husband is one of the men who've gone with your brothers."

Meg nodded. Will's brother-in-law Tom was one of the strongest men of the village; it would make sense for him to ride out. "Who is left to guard us, should anything happen?"

"I am, Meg." Ben's voice broke into their conversation, as he entered the room from the outer wooden steps, looking back on himself to check they were secured, but easy to remove if necessary, and pushing the door tight shut behind him. The steps were hardly used, but could still prove a weak point if the worst happened. "Not just me, don't worry. You have twenty of us at your service. We're putting everyone on alert, ready to come into the enclosure should it be needed."

"Do you expect it to be so?"

"I don't think so. The Elliots have hit Fourtracks again, I think, but there's no reason for them to strike us. We've made our payments, after all."

Meg grimaced at the fuss she had tried to make over

the payment to the Elliots last week. Fourtracks had been struck again, meaning they must have refused to pay, whereas Long Ridge, having paid their dues, had survived the night without problems. Their cattle remained in their enclosure, their villagers safely in their beds. No bloodshed. No retribution.

"Will the remaining people of Fourtracks come here?" Will asked. "We'll need to make space for them. It seems things were bad enough when some arrived last year?"

"No, they've gone south, and to Hexham. They won't come here. I don't think Robert would allow it, as much as it pains him to turn them away." With a nod, Ben excused himself to return to his role of checking the safety and preparedness of the village.

"I don't like this," said Meg, turning to Will once Ben had left them, not bothering to hide her concerns. After all, Will was a villager, and part of their community. "If they've taken the stronger men, what if others attack whilst we're alone? Go, go and help Ben. I'm fine here, and if you're thinking of arguing with me, send Hannah up here in your place. But I want all our men ready to protect us if it comes to it." She fixed him with a direct stare, daring him to argue with her. He didn't, instead nodding and making his way out after Ben. Despite their differences, Meg knew that above all he would do what was best for the village and its residents.

A few minutes later, Hannah appeared from where Will had vanished.

"I'm going to go down to Hexham tomorrow for the market," she said, not bothering with preamble. "I want to hear and see for myself what's happened to Fourtracks this time. The daft sods should just pay up, then this wouldn't keep happening."

Meg put her head in her hands. "I don't want to keep paying the Elliots, but what are we supposed to do? Robert will never stop paying them if things like this keep happening to Fourtracks, and the Elliots are useful friends to have. Maybe this is why he's looking to ally us with Cliffside too."

Hannah scoffed. "That Alexander is strong enough to see off the local Elliots, that's for sure, but I wouldn't trust him, not for a moment. If we enter any agreement with him, I'll be watching my back when he's about."

"Have you told Judd how you feel about it?"

"Of course. He never needs to wonder what I think about something."

"As long as we keep reminding our menfolk of our opinions, that will count for something."

Hannah settled herself in the chair across from Meg, pulling a basket of sewing towards them. "Let's just get through today, and then we'll work out what's best for us all."

CHAPTER SEVEN

In the end, their worries for the day came to nothing, the brothers and their party returning home safely just as dusk was beginning to fall across Long Ridge. But the expressions on the men's faces did nothing to allay Will's fears that trouble could be finding its way to Long Ridge in the near future. The Elliots were too close for his liking, and although they were both English families, that didn't necessarily matter in the borderlands. In times of hardship English attacked English just as much as they attacked Scot, and vice versa. Nobody was secure. The talk of Gray and his men supporting them, and giving them extra strength, set him on edge. The last thing he wanted was for the place he now called home, wanted to keep calling home, to rely on that monster for anything like a level of safety.

He watched Robert leap up the steps two at a time, rushing to Meg's side to assure her that all was well.

For now, thought Will. He hated the look of relief which flooded Meg's face, the sense of happiness that settled comfortably across the village, as people made their way towards the bastle for the evening's feasting, to give everyone something happier to discuss than what had happened at Fourtracks. Only one person seemed to have the same level of concern he was showing: Hannah. Slowly, Will made his way around the room, nodding and smiling as politely as he could, until he reached her. A gentle touch on the shoulder was enough to draw her attention.

"Will? Everything well? Is it Meg?" Her eyes darted around the room, clearly trying to find her friend.

"No, not Meg. This." He gestured to the room. "Do you still plan to go to market tomorrow?"

"To Hexham, yes. I want to find out for myself. Oh, it's not that I don't trust Robert and Judd, but who says what news they've gathered is the right news? I have my own sources. I'll speak to them, and see what they say of what's happened."

"Will you tell me?"

"I'll tell who needs telling, young man. What special interest is it to you?"

"I want to know whether we really need Gray and his Cliffside muscle to protect ourselves."

Hannah's face softened. "You really do not like Gray, do you? Whenever Cliffside is mentioned, in any context, you stiffen. Ah, yes, there you go again. You think nobody sees it, but believe me, I see everything, my pet, everything. I don't know what has happened, and I don't need to, but believe me, if I had my way, there would be no liaising with that man. Him and his men are thugs, if you ask me."

"I could not agree more," said Will. "These problems with the Elliots around here are just going to make it worse, aren't they?"

"Don't think on it too much, laddie." She put a comforting hand on his arm, but he wasn't convinced. "Meg is doing her best to keep us all steady too, don't forget that."

"How much can she truly do, though, if the likes of Robert, Elliot and Gray decide on one path or another?"

Hannah smiled, her eyes back on Meg. "Far more than

you would think, believe you me."

Will wasn't convinced. Yes, Meg was one of the more sensible women, one who knew her own mind, but what would this mean in terms of overall strategy? Would her brothers really listen to her? He watched her now, deep in conversation with Robert. It was too frustrating, having made it all this way away from the troubles of his youth, to end up potentially so involved again. For a moment, he contemplated whether he should just give in and move on again. He knew people in so many places, even over the border. It would be hazardous initially, with the risk of being accused of double-flagging, but if it got him away from here, it might just be worth it.

Then he heard her laugh.

That fluttering, annoying, lively, ridiculous laugh. That laugh he hadn't heard all day, despite it being such a feature of the bastle, on days when she wasn't worried about her friends and family, or the outcome of a raid, or the wellbeing of any particular individual or animal.

Will grimaced. If only she hadn't scared poor Patience that night, everything would be so easy. He could walk away, not look back, send his love in a letter to Cecily, and never see any of the Mathers again for the rest of his life. But thanks to that one stupid moment, the woman had some crazy hold over him, however much he resented her for it. And so of course he wouldn't leave. But one thing was certain: he would never have anything to do with Alexander Gray.

CHAPTER EIGHT

Meg was relieved to hear Hannah's reports of the Fourtracks incident on her return from market the next day. Having both sides of the story calmed her somewhat, despite still being furious that her family had found itself tied to such a deal with the Elliots. Long Ridge would go untouched, with a degree of protection, if they paid their monthly blackmail, but if truth be told it was money which they could ill afford. Reiving families were rarely cash-wealthy, as all their money was tied up in property, land, crops or animals. Some managed to build up suitable levels of income, but generally not through the most legal of manners.

She laughed at herself. Legal? Hardly anything they did was legal, she thought, as she glanced towards the barn and field, half-filled with animals they had reared, half with those they had acquired by one means or another. Sighing, she played with the sleeve of her gown: the gown she had sewn from a bolt of fabric Judd had appeared with following a Day of Truce some years back, where he had sworn he would do nothing untoward, only observe the happenings. Until some deal had been struck for the freedom of a Scot who had wronged them and their neighbours. Hence one bolt of gorgeously soft and warm fabric. A legal lifestyle would be something very strange to her, she thought. She wasn't sure how she would cope.

Her brothers were stalking across the enclosure's open space towards where she was perched on a low bench, their faces dark.

"News?"

Robert shook his head. "No news, that's partly the problem. We were expecting the Warden to be passing through today. It would have been good to be able to speak to him, and see what his thoughts are on the Fourtracks situation."

"I think we know what his thoughts would be," muttered Judd, keeping his eyes fixed on the horizon, as though by doing so he could summon the Warden.

"Even so, speaking to him in person would be of benefit to us all."

Meg nodded. "Let's hope he passes by soon enough. Will we be going to Carlisle for their Day of Truce?" The upcoming event was at the forefront of her mind, having been considering her attire.

The brothers glanced at each other.

"What? What is it now?"

"Gloucester, it seems, is proving effective. Developing the castle over there, by all accounts. We were thinking we would stay away for now, keeping our heads down, whilst the West Marches gets itself sorted out. We have nothing which needs resolving, and if anyone from the west was responsible for the mess at Fourtracks, I would rather be nowhere near."

"Will the West Marches ever be sorted out, even with the king's own brother in charge?" Meg asked. It was worrying, though, having royal authority so evidently present in their midst. So many of their Wardens had been ineffective, either through weakness or their own corruption in the post. But a royal duke amongst them? That could be a whole other matter. He would either be the most corrupt of all, taking advantage of his almost untouchable position, or utterly straight, and actually intending to resolve the issues of his region. She wasn't entirely sure which was the better option for her family, but right now, having a witness nearby would certainly be of benefit. "Why don't you send Ben over? He won't stand out, and can see the lie of the land for us."

Robert grinned. "We are ahead of you there, little sister. Or at least I am. I've asked Lizzie to send him over when he appears from wherever he is currently hiding."

The two men continued on their way, leaving Meg contemplating where Ben might be lurking.

It didn't take her long to spot him. As she sat enjoying a brief moment's peace, she heard more footsteps approaching from outside the enclosure. Ben and Will. The pair were almost inseparable when Will wasn't assisting her. The two men appeared to spot her at the same moment she saw them.

"Meg, greetings to you! I hear your brothers are looking for me?" Ben bowed ridiculously grandly for the occasion.

"They are. They are in need of your service, dear Ben, so best be quick about it," she replied, pulling her hand away as he attempted to kiss it.

He grimaced at her in mock disappointment, then was on his way.

"Join me?" Meg glanced up at Will and gestured to the space beside her.

He shrugged, and dropped heavily onto the stone seat.

"Well, if it is too much of an inconvenience for you, you don't need to stay." She pulled her skirts away from where they touched the sheath of his sword, making a show of not wanting any part of them in contact with the other.

"No inconvenience, but nothing to say, I fear. We've been tending to the animals all morning, and I suspect you're more informed on matters here than I am." Will gestured with a nod to the bastle.

"Just silence then," Meg replied, leaning back against the brick. "I have a bad feeling there'll be precious little of it these coming months."

She watched him from the corner of her eye, as he too leaned back, but not truly relaxing. His back remained straight, his eyes focused on the horizon. She still wasn't sure she entirely understood this young man, or how she felt about him, but in that moment, the silence was perfect.

CHAPTER NINE

November 1471

With her ankle gradually becoming stronger after a couple of weeks, the need for Will to be constantly at Meg's side wasn't as great as it had been, his help only being needed to move her between the levels of the bastle, and occasionally outside, if the mood and weather worked in her favour. With winter drawing in, such chances were limited.

Sitting on the low window seat in the main hall of the bastle one morning, she found herself watching Will as he sparred with Ben, both practising some new manoeuvre to try to bring down a mounted raider as he sped past. Neither had progressed to using actual horses as yet, for fear of harming a valuable animal, and the part of their enemy was played by a high wooden bench fashioned from spare beams.

Seemingly beyond her control, Meg fumed at herself as she felt her heart lurch each time Will was 'beaten' by his opponent, even if the fall was softened by borrowed mattresses and piles of hay.

Then he spotted her at the window, and grinned. That open, boyish grin he had, despite the fact that she knew he had witnessed death, potentially even caused it himself on one of their raids. The grin that, frustratingly, was starting to grow on her. Life at Long Ridge would be so much more simple if she could go back to feeling nothing for Will Hetherington, if he could be just another of Robert and Judd's men, like Ben, whom she could watch fall off the false horse a dozen times, and not feel anything other than concern for an injury she would no doubt have to tend to if it became too serious. Her feelings for Will were becoming far too complicated: torn between wanting to throttle him with her bare hands, and allowing those same hands to wander where they really shouldn't.

She shook her head, trying to physically dislodge the idea of hands being anywhere at all. His had certainly found a way to wander, so subtly that even she hadn't been sure the first time it happened, lingering just half a moment longer than absolutely necessary in the small of her back as he helped her settle into a chair, or holding her foot in place on the step as she tried to climb down herself, when a simple guiding touch would have been more than sufficient. But it was nothing that she would raise with her brothers, partly because it hadn't been entirely unpleasant.

And now he was grinning at her again. Following his friend's line of sight, Ben too looked up to her at the window, and the two men bowed to her, as though about to engage in combat for entertainment's sake.

Ignoring the two below her, for a moment, she let her mind drift to the romanticism of the English court, about which she had only heard snippets of gossip from the Wardens, or others who had been to London and who had stopped off in Hexham on their way between England and Scotland. Tales of grand masked balls, costumes glistening with cloth of gold, everyone adorned in the finest of jewels and gems, practically shining at parties and banquets which could last all day, and indeed most of the night, with plays, music and dancing. They had their feasts now and then at Long Ridge, and there were odd visits to neighbours (or there had been in the past, before things became more violent), but never on a scale such as those at court.

In truth, they had greater proximity to King James in Scotland, and his great events in the likes of Edinburgh and Stirling, than those in London, but both were equally out of reach. She sighed, staring down at her gown, suddenly very aware of how drab it must look, despite it being one of her favourites. Cloth of gold was not for the likes of Meg Mathers.

By the time she looked at the window again, Ben and

Will appeared to have tired of their training, and were sharpening their knives, enjoying the brief respite the afternoon was bringing them, despite the harsh chill in the air.

"Meg, there you are!" Hannah's voice completely erased all traces of her courtly imaginings.

"Hannah, my dear friend, I haven't moved since you walked through an hour ago, I cannot have been so difficult to find," Meg chided, a broad smile on her face. The look on Hannah's soon darkened her thoughts. "What is it?"

"Judd's been summoned to Carlisle, next week, for the Day of Truce."

"Summoned? Why? Is he being accused of something?"

"No, but almost as bad," Hannah said, sitting beside Meg, her hands blindly pulling the cloth she was holding back and forth. "When he was in Hexham, last month, there was an incident."

"The fight he witnessed? Yes, he mentioned it. I didn't think it had been serious?"

"It wasn't at the time, but with all this business over at Fourtracks, the Warden has decided to make an example of things."

"But Judd definitely wasn't involved, was he? I mean, he was telling us the truth when he said he had simply walked out of the tavern and seen the brawl happening across the street?" Meg took Hannah's hands in hers, and looked her in the eye. "Was he lying, so that Robert wouldn't berate him?"

Judd had had his wild days, that was for sure, and his younger self had been part of more brawls than Robert had dared to count, but recently, he genuinely seemed to have been calmer, more mature, and less prone to getting involved with the disputes of the younger generation.

"I asked him outright, and don't you worry, Meggie, I know by now if he's lying to me or not. He's witness to it only, but it's bad enough. You know witnesses are just as prone to trouble if there's folk with a mind for it."

Meg nodded. Plenty of witnesses to crimes had encountered 'accidents' on their way to Days of Truce – or, having provided evidence against somebody, on their return home, if judgements had gone the opposite way to how some would have preferred. At least Judd would only be attending the Middle March's Day of Truce, and not heading to the west, given Robert's decision to stay away from that area until things had calmed down further. Although still a precarious place at times, the Middle March tended to be less violent than the parts to the west and east. Meg hoped it would continue to be the case.

CHAPTER TEN

On the day of Judd's summoning, the Long Ridge men were out in force, determined to put on a show of strength, should anything arise during the session. On the ride to the Reidswire, there had been little sign of trouble – little sign of anything at all, in fact – and it had felt almost like a pleasant ride out in the country.

Will and Ben rode side by side behind the two Mathers brothers, enjoying the sun, but maintaining their levels of alertness, should they inadvertently fall into a cleverly-placed trap or ambush. It wouldn't be the first time a Day of Truce had been used in such a way.

Patience was playing the part of her name beautifully, meandering along the well-trodden paths. The group were keen to make sure they were visible, not wanting to give any indication of this being anything other than what it truly was: an escort to ensure Judd was able to make his allotted summons. He would arrive just before the stated time, do what needed to be done, then leave, his reputation as an honest man amongst the reivers intact.

That was the plan.

Will was the first to see Alexander Gray, at the head of his own retinue, riding into the village, coming along the road in the opposite direction to the men of Long Ridge. Despite the ongoing communications between Robert and Alexander, the two men had only met briefly once so far, and Will, thankfully, hadn't been present. It was over a decade since he had encountered the man, but he hadn't changed one bit. He seemed, fittingly, to be entirely dark, from his shoulder-length black hair, the black material of his outfit, and even a jet-black horse: entirely at odds with the Mathers brothers' appearance, in blue and brown jackets over white shirts, their dark-brown hair kept shorter, neater, making their relationship even more obvious, drawing attention to their almost-identical noses, and the blue-grey eyes, the same as Meg's.

For a moment, Will paused, almost pulled back on Patience's reins, then realised that would make him stand out more than if he just carried on as expected. After all, there was no reason to suggest Gray would recognise him, or even remember the incident which had been burned into Will's memory for almost half his lifetime.

The raiding of his family's village, the destruction of his home, the murder of his parents. He could still hear their screams.

Seeing Gray brought it all back, piercing through his mind as though it had happened only yesterday. At least Cecily would be spared the shock of it. If Gray ever came to Long Ridge, Will and Tom would make sure Cecily was pre-warned, and knew what was coming. But that was in the future. At this moment, Will had to pull himself together and keep control of his temper. He couldn't afford to do anything to disrupt Robert's plans, even if those plans did include the monster who had killed his family.

"Gray!" It was Judd who spoke first, calling their distant neighbour over to their group.

"Mathers, what are you here for? Mixed up in this stupid fight business too? I hope your men weren't amongst the brawlers?"

"No, not ours, Judd is a witness only," Robert answered for them both, as the two brothers turned and steadied their horses. "You?"

"A misjudged accusation states that one of my own, Hal, was part of the fight. I'm here to convince them otherwise." Alexander's fist tightened on the hilt of his sword. "It should be easy enough. I presume you didn't see Hal Robson as part of the pack, Judd?"

Will watched as Judd paused for a moment, glancing subtly at Robert. Almost imperceptibly, the leader of Long Ridge shrugged. Will kept his eye on the older brother. An

Englishman with a Scottish name, he was as one with Hal, the randomness of the borders bringing Scots and English far closer than some would like. But that, it seemed, was where the similarity ended. Judd believed in fairness and honour, even if it was only amongst thieves.

"I remember clearly what I saw that day, Gray. But luckily for your man, if he was there, he wasn't in my eye line."

"And what of your other men?"

"I was on my own that day. I had ridden into town on personal business; there was nobody with me."

Gray nodded, seemingly satisfied with the outcome. Or this one at least. "Excellent. Let us hope everyone else is as agreeable."

Will kept his head down as the Cliffside men rode on past, glad to be insignificant enough not to be noticed. He was just another youngster, riding in the middle of the pack. There was no reason for Gray to single him out.

"Was Hal there?" Robert was asking Judd, as soon as Gray was out of hearing.

Judd shook his head. "He wasn't in the brawl as far as I saw. But he was in Hexham that day, that's for sure. I just hope for their sake that any other witnesses agree with Gray, or their life won't be worth living."

The two brothers watched as Gray paused again in the distance, having encountered another group arriving along the street. They winced at the sound of metal on metal, as swords were drawn.

CHAPTER ELEVEN

"I ask you again, Judd Mathers, of Long Ridge: did you see the man in question, the man standing in front of you, taking part in the brawl last month?"

The Warden of the Middle March was standing directly in front of Judd, as though trying to intimidate him into seeing things his way. Judd didn't flinch. "And I tell you again, Sir: no, I did not. I saw the fight, and have told you who I saw taking part, but Hal was not one of them."

Shoulders slumped, the Warden dismissed Judd from his place in front of the council. Will looked on as Gray and his men stood tall, awaiting Hal's dismissal from his place at the other side of the room. Witness after witness had agreed with Gray's version of events, and now there was nothing the Warden could do other than to release his man.

Judd rejoined the Long Ridge group, standing beside Robert and Will. "I don't like this. I know what I saw, but Gray must have got to some of the others. They looked terrified."

"But if you didn't see him, maybe he is actually innocent?" suggested Robert, his voice low to match his brother's.

"No, you know his reputation. If there was a fight, he would have been there, right in the middle of things. We need to watch things here, Rob, and keep Gray sweet. He's managed to turn everyone today, but imagine how bad things might get if he fails one day. Think of Fourtracks."

"You think he was involved?"

"There's no evidence, or the Warden would have hauled Gray himself up there. I think it was the Scots, as everyone is saying, but Gray could still have been involved, identifying a weakened target after all they've been through. It's a nice new sword belt he's wearing today, don't you think, and a fine steed he rode in on."

Will looked closely at the man he had been trying to avoid all day. He certainly was dressed more finely than any other man present, including the Warden. Even when times were good, few reivers would have wasted money on such finery, when defences could be strengthened, or provisions built up for when things turned against them. Compared to Gray, the Mathers brothers looked almost shabby.

He looked down at his own clothes, dull in shades of brown and fading black. They were clean, and practical, but could never be described as smart, however hard he tried. Unwillingly, his mind drifted to Meg. Despite himself, he found himself wondering which style of man she would she prefer. Smart, showy, but hiding darkness underneath, or honest, but close to being worn out? Will found himself hoping for the latter, as Robert called the men together and they began the ride back to Long Ridge.

***

Meg was waiting for the men as they rode into the enclosure that evening, having made her way slowly down through the bastle with Cecily's help. Hannah and Lizzie had joined the waiting party, making the most of the relatively warm and dry evening.

"A welcome sight indeed, ladies," called Robert, jumping down from his horse and greeting his sister with a kiss on the cheek.

"How was it?" Meg asked, her arms on his.

"As expected," replied Judd.

"It's true, and nothing further to report," agreed Robert, nodding to his brother.

"Nothing further?" Meg wasn't satisfied with the answers she had been given.

"Nothing of note happened, Meg," said Will, as he escaped Cecily's fond embrace. "I'm sure we can recount everything in more detail later, but for now, I think we could all do with a rest."

Her brothers agreed, Robert requesting hot water, and Judd making his way out to the village, hand-in-hand with Hannah. Before Will and Ben could vanish as easily, Meg held them back.

"Nothing further to report?" she repeated.

Ben sighed. "Whether Hal was there or not, Gray made it clear that 'innocent' was the only outcome which would be acceptable. The man is dangerous, but your brothers have agreed to keeping him on side for now, albeit with one eye on each other's backs."

Without another word, the men each retreated to their respective homes.

CHAPTER TWELVE

Lying on his small pallet bed that night, Will found sleep difficult to achieve. Once again, Alexander Gray had got his own way in a situation where he must have been at fault. Otherwise, why make such a big show of tracking down the witnesses and making sure they knew what to say? The man hadn't changed a bit; that much was clear. And now Will would be forced to ride alongside him as an ally, even if only for the occasional raid. He knew that no good could come of it.

A noise outside the window brought him from his thoughts. Somebody was out and about, but in the middle of the night? The sound of a woman's gasp of pain shook away the last fog of tiredness, and in a heartbeat he was out of bed, reaching for the short sword he always kept close at hand. Tom and Cecily were still fast asleep as he crept past their curtained bed and out of the small wooden door of the cottage.

It was her. Meg. With small, careful steps, she was making her way from the enclosure, out towards the village. What he had heard first must have been the sound of the gate opening. A flash of irritation surged through him; what on earth was she doing, out and about at this hour? And where was she going, that she didn't want to be observed? It couldn't be anything her brothers approved of, Will thought, not taking his eyes off her even as he slipped open the door and moved past it in silence. If she was up to something, it didn't matter that she was his master's sister – the village's protection was his first concern.

Staying in the shadows, he watched, waiting for her to draw level with him, planning to stay behind her as she went to wherever she was going. For a terrible moment, he wondered whether she was about to betray them all to Gray. Not that he had seen any evidence that this was possible, but really, what did he know of her? He tried to force the thought from his mind – Meg was the most fiercely loyal member of the Long Ridge community he had met. She couldn't be about to let them all down.

He realised she hadn't drawn level with him at all, although even at her slow pace, she should have reached him by now. Leaning forward, he saw that she was heading back to the bastle, using a stick to take as much of her weight as she could. Hobbling onwards, whatever she had been planning, had she changed her mind? He shadowed her, keeping to the darkness, and watching his step, so she wouldn't suddenly hear him and be startled.

The animals in the barn hadn't had the same warning. A sudden shudder from the barn drew Meg's attention at just the wrong moment, as she lifted her hand to let herself back into the gate, and she dropped the stick she had been using to support her. Will suspected he saw what was about to happen before Meg had realised, as she was caught off-guard, and almost toppled. He reached her before she fell, wrapping his arms around her, steadying her, before she could find her own footing.

"What the hell are you doing out here?" he hissed at her. "Where were you going?"

Anger flashed across her face, even in the moonlight. "I could ask you the same questions."

"But I asked them first, and I'm armed," Will replied.

"You dare to threaten me?"

"No, of course not, but just tell me what you're up to. Do your brothers know you're out here?"

Her shoulders slumped, and he loosened his grip, helping her lean more comfortably against the wall.

"I needed to practise walking, without being fussed over."

He narrowed his eyes at her, then followed her gaze to her ankle, and the truth dawned on him. "You've been coming down here every night, just to try and build your strength up?"

"Not every night, but when I've felt strong enough. I've been feeling like a prisoner in my own home. Will, do you know how that feels for somebody like me?"

He shook his head.

"I know it isn't exactly normal for around here, but my brothers have always valued my input, with the farming as well as the raids. I've ridden out with them to check on our livestock and crops, such as they are. I've spent time with everyone on the lands we control, and done everything with them, side-by-side. And yet here I am, stuck at home, incapable of doing anything."

"But it isn't permanent, you know that. Another couple of weeks, and you'll be back on your feet; another month or two, it'll be as though nothing ever happened," Will argued, trying to point out the obvious to her.

"What if they stop needing me?"

Will sighed, and despite himself, drew her close for an embrace. "For somebody so bright, you can be ridiculous," he said, hoping she wouldn't see his smile in the darkness.

"Ridiculous?" Meg tried to push back, but he simply held her more tightly.

"You are injured, and out of action for what, two months, maximum? During that time, you've been writing letters, as usual, checking the accounts, as usual, speaking to tenants and villagers, as usual, keeping an eye on everything, as usual. The only thing you haven't been able to do is get on a horse and go out to people. Have you noticed what's been happening instead? Well?" He looked down at her, forcing her to respond.

Meg shook her head, a sullen pout forming on her face.

"People have been coming to you. They haven't been ignoring you, they've been getting on their own horses and coming here instead. Does that not tell you something? So stop feeling sorry for yourself, keep on doing what you're doing, and don't you dare come out here like this again, on your own. What would have happened if you had made it out of the village, and fallen? We might not have found you for days."

"I've never even gone past the first cottages," Meg mumbled.

"It doesn't matter. You're forgetting something else here. I'm supposed to be looking after you, so what happens if you're injured again? Whether I'm with you or not, you can guarantee your brothers will find a way of blaming me. Think on that too, won't you?"

Meg nodded. "I just hate feeling so useless."

"You're anything but useless. Come on, let's get you back inside."

"No! I mean, not yet. Can we stay, get some air, enjoy the stillness? It wasn't a pleasant evening, with Robert and Judd fuming about Gray's behaviour today."

Will tensed at the mention of Gray's name. She must have felt it, he thought, as he battled to control his emotions.

"What is it?" she asked.

"Men… like him. They trouble me, if you must know. Men who take power as though it's their right, not something to be earned."

"Like Robert?"

"Exactly. He has earned the respect he has. Gray just expects it, and destroys anyone who stands in his way." He inhaled deeply. "Come on, enough talk of him. Let's get you settled so you can get the weight off that ankle."

Luckily, she took his hint, and they sat without any further mention of Gray.

CHAPTER THIRTEEN

That situation didn't last for long; she had to know what he was thinking.

"What did you mean by 'men like him'?" Meg asked, once they had been sitting for a while, enjoying the stillness of the night. Despite the darkness, she turned to face him. "Where have you encountered it before?"

Will sighed. "My parents. They died, as a result of a man like Gray."

"Tell me?" she asked, softly, moving herself closer to him, in encouragement and comfort.

"There was a raid, an unlucky attack. We weren't ready. We had just been victim to a Scots raid, and we saw him, a powerful landowner, riding towards us one evening. You know, we didn't even ready ourselves for defence; we thought the Warden had sent him, perhaps, to give a show of protection, of strength. It was quite the opposite." Will paused, twisting the cord of his shirt around his fingers. "When he reached us, we realised things were bad. They didn't slow down. They had these huge torches, and they began setting the turf cottages ablaze. We were being destroyed, only days after we thought we were recovering from the worst we would ever have to face. We had no livestock, the crops were burned, all we had were our homes, and he took those, along with any valuables he and his thugs could lay their hands on. Our father died trying to save us, but he couldn't stop them taking our mother…"

Meg reached for Will's hand, as she heard his voice begin to crack. "It's alright, you don't have to continue."

Will shook his head. "No, it's good to say it. Cecily won't talk of it to me. We were in our early teens – little more than children. They took our mother, but we should have known there was no chance of a ransom being demanded; we had no means to pay it anyway. We found her the next morning, dead in a ditch at the side of the track. No doubt when they realised she was of no use to them, she was just left. It was winter, she wouldn't have had a chance."

Without thinking, Meg reached up and put her arm around Will's shoulder, realising he was shaking with silent tears. "I am so sorry. I truly am. Cecily never told us any of this."

"She wouldn't. We were separated after that night. She was taken to Hexham, and I set out to try and find my own way. It was only when I realised the only sensible thing was to join her, that I sought her out here. Happily, she and Tom were willing and able to take me in, and your brothers have been so kind. Nobody's ever tried to pry too deeply."

"So that's where she met Tom," mused Meg. "I've always found them such a good match for each other."

"She's happy here, and when I saw that, I thought I might as well try my hand at being happy here too." Will leaned down to fix the lacing on his boot, and extricated himself from her arm.

"And are you?"

He paused, looking out across the darkness to the village. There were no candles or lanterns burning at this hour, with even the bastle dark. "Yes, I think so, mostly. Out there, on the moors, either keeping our own cattle, or where necessary taking those of others, that's where I belong. I was raised for it, and at least here I have somebody to care for again."

Meg looked at him sharply. "You do?"

"Well of course. Having Cecily here has given me a sense of purpose again."

She closed her eyes for a moment, breathing in deeply. Of course he didn't mean her, and had she really wanted him to think that anyway? Moving casually away from him, under the pretence of checking the lace of her boot, she nodded.

"Siblings are always a great source of support. Come on," she said, sitting up again. "As you've disturbed my walk, you might as well help me back up to the main room. I've been getting as far as there, and stopping, letting them think all I can manage is down one set of stairs, in case they worry about me."

She held out her hand, knowing he would help her. He might be able to tease her, but at least she was finding out more each day about William Hetherington and his past.

CHAPTER FOURTEEN

December 1471

"Come on, Meg, today's the day," Will's voice was full of forced cheer as Hannah pulled back the curtains on Meg's chamber a week later, blinking in the brightness of the winter sun glinting on the frost outside.

"He has a point. You did say that today you would make the effort, get out of the village even," Hannah added, pouring warmed water into a low basin for her friend.

Meg grumbled and rolled over, her face to the wall. It had been a restless night, and the last thing she wanted was to have to put in even more effort to show how hard she was trying. Her ankle was improving; she could tell that. Just the previous night, with Will's support, she had managed to hop herself up the wooden stairs to her bedchamber, but the exertion had taken the energy out of her, and this morning she just wanted to sleep, forgetting the promises she had made.

So an hour later it was not the happiest version of Meg which Will helped to make her way out of the bastle's enclosure, and onto the main track between the houses of Long Ridge.

"Where are we going?" he asked her, as they finally reached the final cottage in the row, an arm placed carefully in the small of her back, the other hand holding hers in support, as though they were about to begin a country dance.

She glanced upwards, instinctively, to the low rise above the village. Her spot. The place she had been running away to since she was old enough to escape the watchful eyes of her parents and guardians, even of her brother.

Will followed her gaze, and sighed. "Really? You don't

think a hill might be a bit too ambitious for your first walk out of the village? I was just thinking to the end of the final cottage and back, depending on how you went."

It was enough to push her out of her bad mood, and into fury. "Too ambitious? Too ambitious! How dare you? If I want to go to my favourite place in this hellish world, I shall do so. And if you have to help me, then that is your fault for allowing this to happen in the first place."

He removed both his arm and hand from their supporting positions, and for a heartbeat, she felt herself shake unsteadily, but she didn't care. Grabbing his sword from its sheath, it became her improvised walking stick, as she wobbled carefully a few steps away from him. With each additional step, although the pain threatened to grow, her determination grew more quickly. There was no way she was letting this man, the one who had caused her to be out of action when she was most needed by her family, see how much effort it was taking to move one foot in front of the other without showing the pain.

She had hardly moved more than ten feet by the time he snapped out of his shock and moved to catch up with her. "What the hell do you think you're doing? You don't just take a man's sword from him! That is a deadly weapon."

"A deadly weapon I am perfectly capable of using, whether as a sword or a stick," she retorted. She had made it to twenty feet now, her pace gradually increasing as her fury fired her onwards, burying the pain in anger. Yes, it was a steep path, but a solid one, up the small incline behind the last cottage, to a wide flat rock at bench height, always conveniently shielded from view (even in winter) by the sturdy vegetation in front of it.

Her place. Another push, another hundred feet or so forward, and she would be there. Whether he liked it or not. She hoped.

"Do you think I'm going to simply stand here and let you climb a hill you're very clearly not going to make it up, or even if you do, which you are bound to fall down on your way back?" Despite his words, he wasn't making any attempt to catch her up again; Meg could hear that he had stopped.

"I don't care what you think. And clearly you don't care what I think either, so why don't we just stop the pretence? I don't need you here, either now or at any other moment. I proved that much last night. So why don't you simply pass me that branch, take back your sword, and be about your business?" She gestured to the sturdy stick she could see, but which was just slightly out of reach for her, but refused to turn to face him, refused to back down.

"No."

"What?"

"No. You can either get the stick yourself, or come back here, and I'll escort you back to the bastle. Once you're back there, I am finished with this task. There'll be no more running and fetching, or waiting on you like a page. You are clearly content that you can manage, so you can tell your brothers that you have dismissed me. And all of this is over. We can both go back to the lives we very much prefer – each without the other in it."

For a moment, Meg didn't speak. She blinked at him, twice, expecting the words to come, but none did. Then she felt the anger rising within her, from the pit of her stomach where it had spent so much of the last few weeks balled up, ready to rush out, just waiting for the right moment. Without another thought, she spun on her good heel.

"I'll take care of myself then, so can have the bloody sword back, see if I care! You've been nothing but a burden and a hindrance, which is clearly how you see me too, so that's it. I am going this way, and you shall go that. I would rather I didn't see you again, as unlikely a wish that may be."

She turned again, more slowly this time, back along the path she had been following. Hot tears stung her eyes, threatening her vision, but she pushed them out of the way, even more determined now to reach that wretched rock. It wasn't even important, but suddenly, it was imperative that she make it to the place which had been her sanctuary for so much of her life. Aware she still carried his sword, she flung it behind her, not caring to see where it landed.

His gasp of pain stopped her in her tracks.

Scared, almost, to see what damage she had inflicted, she didn't move for a heartbeat, concentrating so hard on the ground in front of her. So hard that she didn't hear his footsteps rushing to catch up with her; didn't realise he was directly behind her until she felt his hand pulling on hers, turning her to face him.

The sight of the blood jolted her. His hand was damp and red. Instinctively, she reached out for it. The logical part of her brain was even now assessing the wound, telling her that it was nothing, just an unlucky scratch; that she had seen wounds a hundred times worse in her time at the bastle, and that Will would hardly even notice the mark it left behind in a couple of days; that it wasn't his sword hand. But her heart was racing. Will instinctively closed his hand, wincing with the pain, their fingers entwining, as his other arm snaked back around her waist. He wasn't holding her up this time though, he was pulling her closer, his hand dropping hers now, to pull her closer still, his lips coming down to meet hers as she turned her face upwards without even realising what she was doing.

Until he stopped. His breath warmed her cool lips as he leaned forward, foreheads together, his eyes closed, but in sadness or anger, she couldn't quite tell.

"Don't you dare stop there, William Hetherington."

His eyes snapped open, there was a hint of a smile, then their lips met.

In a moment, the weeks of frustrated attraction burst free from them both, as their hands wandered, taking in the shape of the other, newly exploring, despite so long in close proximity, finally giving in to what had been building since that fateful night. After a heartbeat too long, Will pulled away from Meg, holding her face in his hands, forcing him to meet her eyes.

"We can't, Meg, we can't." His breath was quick, as he released her from his grip and took a step backwards.

"But Will…" Meg started to reply, but he already had his back to her, and was now walking away far too quickly for her to attempt to catch up. Stranded, she watched him vanish around the corner of the first cottage, leaving her truly alone for the first time in weeks.

Suddenly furious at what had happened, she turned and limped towards her rock, her heart racing despite her fresh melancholy. Within minutes, she saw Will heading towards the bastle, and exiting with Patience, before racing her out of the village in the opposite direction. Meg doubted she would see him again that day.

CHAPTER FIFTEEN

Meg's prediction held, although whether by design or chance, she wasn't sure. There was a raid planned for that night. It was a show of strength more than anything, before the weather closed in for the season, but a foray over the border nonetheless. With her ankle still weak, Meg was dispatched to the upper floor of the bastle when the men returned. There would be no risking a repeat of the previous incident; no presence for her at all until she was fully healed. Robert had declared so.

She watched Will ride back into the enclosure, thankfully intact, but she wasn't able to see his face clearly, and had no idea who, if anyone, had tended to his wound. Her wound, she thought bitterly. She should have seen it coming, should have known better than to throw a weapon, even without her full weight behind it. But (not for the first time) her anger had got the better of her.

Once all had been settled, whether in barns or beds, she sought out Hannah. She found her clearing away from where the men had shared a cup of ale in the main hall after the raid.

"Has everyone returned safe and well?" she asked, settling by the fire, and pouring them both a cup, gesturing for her friend to join her.

"Ben has a nasty gash on his arm. An arrow came too close for my liking, but he'll certainly live. And Michael fell from horse on the way home and got himself a nice bruise to impress the ladies with, all down his left side. But again, he'll live. And your Will—"

"Not my Will," Meg interrupted.

"Alright, just 'Will' then, has a cut on his hand, not sure where that's come from. Looks fresh, from today certainly, but he won't say what caused it, and nobody saw anything happen to him. It's clean, anyway, that's the main thing. He'll be right enough, and now with a handsome scar to show off about. He'll look a proper warrior." She took a deep sip from the ale. "And your brothers are well. Nothing to worry about there."

Meg wasn't thinking of her brothers; for once, news of their safe return was of secondary importance to her. If Hannah hadn't tended Will's wound, then it must have been Cecily. That was a relief. His sister was competent, having helped in the bastle on plenty of occasions. There would be no infection to worry about, but she suspected that having scarred the young man would make him even angrier with her.

Winter at Long Ridge was looking to be a long difficult season, although at least there was plenty of food in their stores and cattle in their barns, so none of the residents would starve. Those who had stayed at Fourtracks weren't so lucky, with tales of the village being all but abandoned as the final few families had to move on to find sufficient food to get through the months ahead. Hexham was busier than usual, as Hannah reported each week when she visited for the market, selling eggs, or trinkets made by the villagers, or trading for fresh produce as required.

Meg watched as Robert and Judd began the annual ritual of counting their wins of the year, working out what food they had to go around, and at what point they would need to consider rationing measures. It was always the same after the final major raid of the year had taken place: the two brothers, on their own, turning away any offers of help from the other villagers. They had always seen it as their responsibility to ensure everyone would have enough to survive the winter, never letting anyone else take any part of the burden.

The Warden's representative did finally arrive (though without the Warden himself) one bitingly cold Sunday afternoon, as they had all returned from the chapel in the village. They had shivered as the priest delivered his sermon, before retreating to his warmed house in the neighbouring valley – which, as with so many, was under the protection of the Elliots.

"Sir, we are glad to have your presence. Won't you join us for a cup of ale, to help ward off this chill?"

The older man, Jarvis, sank heavily into a chair at the table, and drank gratefully from the offered cup before anyone spoke.

"You're the first home to offer me refreshment today, if you can imagine that? On a Sunday too." He glanced hopefully at Hannah, who smiled as she refilled his cup. "In this weather as well."

"You've been visiting a lot today then?" Judd went straight to the heart of the matter, Meg observed. If the Warden's assistant was visiting, then there must be a reason for it.

"There were rumours of violence. English on English, can you believe it? The Grays were suspected, but I cannot find any proof of it, worse luck. They're a hard lot, worse than the Elliots if you ask me. I heard a terrible rumour that you had considered throwing in your lot with them, heading over the border together?" He paused, scanning the brothers' faces. Seemingly disappointed in their lack of reaction, he continued regardless. "Well, anyway, they're trouble if you ask me. If you're involved in any of their ploys, I would watch your back with them, as much as from the Scots."

Evidently sensing he was going to get no further on the topic, Jarvis drained his cup, and moved onto other, less controversial matters. "I see you've plenty of cattle still, awaiting the necessary slaughter, when the time comes?"

Not needing to get involved further, Meg rose from her place, and with Hannah left the men to discuss whatever arose next.

"They're serious then, about joining with Gray?" she demanded, as soon as they were alone.

"I think it's already done. Judd put up some resistance,

but at the end of the day, Gray is too powerful. We'll be joining with them any day now, I imagine." Hannah sounded resigned to the fact.

Meg sighed, and looked out of the window. Life had never been peaceful for them, not with their lifestyle, but she had a feeling things were going to become a lot worse.

CHAPTER SIXTEEN

Wrapped in her warm cloak to protect against the December winds, Meg sat on the low bench against the wall of the bastle, with the smell of Hannah's mutton stew filling her nostrils and making her stomach growl. Despite the cold, she had needed to escape the bastle and the frosty atmosphere which was slowly threatening to overtake them all, with the thought Gray's presence hanging over them. Through the fading light, she could make out somebody approaching, and tensed, her hand moving to where a sword would be (a habit she had never grown out of, since being trained to fight, even if only for fun, as a small girl), when she realised it was Will. It had been over a week since their encounter at the end of the village, and she had still been carefully avoiding him. But her options were limited. Even with her ankle all but healed, there was nowhere for either of them to go, and her travelling beyond the village bounds without a solid escort was out of the question.

He paused for a moment at the gate to the enclosure, as though the sight of her had made him doubt his next move. But perhaps, she thought, the draw of the hot meal was greater than the desire not to spend any time in her company. He approached.

"Good evening," she called, determined to make the first move in whatever game of conversation was about to begin.

He grunted a response, and kept walking.

"We will have to have a conversation eventually, Will, whatever you think of that."

"Then, barring this one, I shall endeavour to keep the risk at bay as long as I am able."

She laughed at the formality of his reply, then brought herself up short. "You regret it?"

"I stopped it, didn't I? So of course I regret it. You are my master's sister, and I do not intend to put my place here at risk because of a stupid mistake. I've been your manservant for long enough now, and it's time to start rebuilding my reputation amongst the villagers, before spring comes and the raids begin again. I would request that you forget what happened between us, and let me get on with that, whilst you get on with your own plans."

"My own plans? You think I have plans? William, I am the sister of a family of reivers, a younger sister at that. As soon as either of my brothers finally decides to do their duty by this family and have a child, I shall have no place here. My only role in life is to live here, caring for my family and villagers, until Robert and Judd decide whoever it is I am to marry – and then, much to my sadness, I will leave Long Ridge and set up home doing exactly the same thing in another village, for another bastle, and another family, until I have either my own son to inherit, or daughter to go through the cycle again. Do not mock me with the idea of having plans." She felt her voice rising, but could do nothing about it.

"But that is the way of the world. You acknowledge that yourself."

"Acknowledge, yes, but accept? Not for a moment. If I had my choice, I would remain here. But since neither of my brothers seem to have any urgent desire to bring an heir into the world, male or female, perhaps that could still happen. Who knows? All I do know is that it is out of my control. You may have choices, and ideas of plans, but I do not."

Will stared at his feet for a moment. "You would stay here?"

"Of course. But not because of you; do not let yourself think that for a moment." Meg surprised herself at the anger in her voice. But it had needed saying. He had hurt her, rushing away that day, after the kiss, the kiss she kept remembering in exquisite detail, and she refused to give him the satisfaction of knowing that the idea of repeating the experience had entered her mind more than once since then.

"I didn't know. Most women don't have a care where they go, as long as it's comfortable."

"Ha!" she scoffed. "You clearly haven't discussed this with Cecily. She has a care, that's how she ended up here, rather than being cast out elsewhere. Long Ridge is a good village to call home. You must have learned that, even in your short time with us. Compare us to the likes of Cliffside. The differences are clear."

He didn't reply.

"I appreciate that this is nothing but a game to you, and I don't even know whether you will be staying with us past the end of the winter, but know this – I love this village, and I have no desire to leave it." She pulled her shawl closer around her, suddenly feeling colder than she could cope with, and waited for him to leave.

Without another word, Will nodded to her, and headed into the bastle.

CHAPTER SEVENTEEN

The claustrophobia of winter didn't help reduce the tension between Meg and Will. There were few raids through the dark, cold months, with most villages closing in on themselves and pulling together to get through the worst of the year. It was difficult to avoid somebody in such close quarters.

Hannah's voice pulled Meg from her thoughts. "Meg, pet, will you take this over to Cecily? She'll need it the way she's feeling."

"Sorry, yes, of course." Without another glance, Meg took the thick woollen blanket from Hannah's arms, added it to the basket of provisions they had been gathering for their friend, currently struck down with a fever. "It will break soon, won't it?"

"She's a strong one, I don't see why it shouldn't. But in the meantime we'll do what we can for her, and keep poor Tom fed, warm and watered."

Cecily's husband had been doing what he could, repaying the kindness they had been shown by helping out even more than usual around the village, but the worry he felt was clear for all to see. With Christmas growing ever closer, and most other families trying to feel more joyful despite their difficulties, it was even harder for Tom.

"I know it's silly, but I've put some sprigs of holly and other greenery in there for them, so he can at least make the house look more festive. You never know whether she'll be alert enough to notice, but if she is, it might cheer her." Hannah put some final items into the basket and handed it to Meg. "Be careful how you go out there."

Meg smiled and made her way slowly down through the bastle and out into the enclosure. The heavy frost of the night before still clung to the ground, but at least it had frozen the muddy ruts which had been steadily developing over the previous weeks. Solid ground was easier for her to pick her way across than mud, and with the stick she had been using, Meg would be at Cecily and Tom's cottage with only a few minutes of effort. Besides, a sore ankle was as nothing compared to what they were going through.

She was already through the door of the small cottage when she noticed a third person in the tiny main chamber of the dwelling. Will. Of course he would be there. She cursed at her own stupidity. With no raids to plan, and their defences as sound as they could be, what else was there for the young men of Long Ridge to do other than stay warm in their family homes? Especially when a beloved family member had spent the last week drifting in and out of consciousness.

"I, um, I brought these," Meg stammered, holding out the basket as though to prove her point.

"Thanks Meg, and to Hannah, well, to everyone up there. You've all been so kind," said Tom, taking the offered gift and setting it on the table. He pulled the blanket out, holding it in his outstretched arms. "Oh no, you must take this back; this is too good to be in a place like this for too long."

"Nonsense. Cecily needs it far more than any of us do at the moment. She's welcome to it."

"Will you have a cup of ale with us?" Tom asked, going to collect his own offering in return for Meg's.

"No, thank you, I must be getting back." To what, Meg wasn't sure, but she knew she couldn't stay in Will's company any longer than necessary.

"Please. It will be good to have some female company, and if she wakes, a friendly face will do her the power of good, I'm sure."

"You're bored, aren't you Tom?" she said, smiling, and nodding her acceptance of the ale.

"Bored and scared," he admitted. He gestured the jug of ale to Will, who still cradled an empty cup of his own, but the younger man shook his head.

"I'll be away for a bit, see if there's anything needing doing," Will said, rising to his feet. "Thanks for the gifts, Meg, I'm sure Cecily will appreciate them."

Meg watched as he went, her eye staying on the door when it swung shut behind him, hoping, despite herself, that he would return.

"Everything well between you two?" Tom asked.

"What? Us two? I mean, sorry?"

"It's just, one moment he's declaring you're the most irritating creature on earth, and then the next, he's worrying about whether you and everyone else will be safe and fed through the winter. He does speak fondly of you, you know."

Meg felt her face warming. "I'm sure he does, but I'm also sure there is nothing in terms of 'us two' for you or anyone else to be worrying about."

"I'm not one for gossip, Meg, you must know that by now. But please do stay a little if you can. There can't be that much for you to be doing up at the bastle."

As far as Meg could think, there really wasn't much that couldn't wait a couple of hours whilst she kept a worried husband and good friend company. Smiling at him, she settled into the chair Will had just vacated, indicating she was content to remain for as long as he wanted to talk.

Over an hour later, a low moan from Cecily broke into Tom and Meg's conversation.

"Cecily!" they both exclaimed in unison, the sense of relief evident in both voices. Their conversation had been friendly, but stilted.

The young woman on the bed groaned again, then her eyes flickered open, as she struggled to focus on the room.

"Don't crowd her," warned Meg, gently holding Tom back, as he jumped up from his seat. "Sit next to her gently, and speak softly. It might help bring her round to us."

It was sound advice, as Tom chattered softly about the

comings and goings of the cottage over the last week, as his beloved wife had slipped in and out of wakefulness. Gradually, Cecily seemed to understand more of what he was saying, as she frowned with the effort of listening, then smiled, as Tom voiced his relief that she was back with him.

"I love you," he said, stroking the hair away from her face.

Speaking was still too much for her, but the small smile on Cecily's face was enough to let Meg know everything would be well. Returning the smile with her own, she slipped out of the door and left them in peace.

CHAPTER EIGHTEEN

None of them saw Tom or Will until the next evening, neither man wanting to leave Cecily's side in case the turn of good fortune were to swing back the other way and take her back into illness. So yet more food was sent over with Lizzie, once they had confirmed that although still weak, Cecily was starting to seem alert to what they were saying. Both men had been given the strictest instructions from Hannah as to how to make sure Cecily was kept hydrated, and she had decided not to crowd them, in case their joy had unexpectedly turned to grief.

Meg had been mulling over Tom's words about Will. She was unsure whether she was pleased that he might be concerned for her wellbeing, or annoyed that he was still being patronising, even now she was almost entirely recovered from her injured ankle. In truth, there was hardly any reason for them to interact at all now, if she didn't want to.

If she didn't want to. There was the decision. As though the world was making the decision for her, she found herself strolling towards the makeshift stables, which were used when the threat of attack was lower, and the animals needed more space than being kept together in the bastle's lower floor.

Stroking the mane of the nearest horse, she was aware of movement nearby.

"Hello?" she called out, cautiously moving away from the horses, keen to avoid another injury if one of the animals were to be spooked again.

"What is it? Something wrong? Oh." Will's questions were silenced as he walked around the wooden divider and came face-to-face with her. "It's you."

"Were you expecting somebody else?"

"I wasn't 'expecting' anyone – I was just using my time

sensibly, looking after the horses. Patience hasn't been out for a couple of days. She needed some caring for, even if I haven't found the time to exercise her."

Meg looked at her feet. "We could go for a ride this afternoon?"

"I'm not sure that's a good idea. Patience needs a good ride out, and I'm not risking going that far with you still not completely fit."

"Oh, so you do care after all?" Meg looked him in the eye, challenging him to reply one way or the other.

Will sighed, his hands on his hips. "Care? Of course I care, but where's that going to get me? We've already agreed that nothing can come of this, however either of us feel. So why put ourselves through any heartache?"

"Heartache?"

"Heartache."

She smiled and took a step forward, closing the gap between them. "I can stand it if you can," she murmured, reaching her arms around his neck.

CHAPTER NINETEEN

The dawning of the Christmas season brought a glimmer of merriment to the dark days of winter at Long Ridge. The markets of Hexham were also busier, with people trying to obtain the best they could with limited supplies to go around, and even more limited supplies of money, but somehow, the Mathers had so far always managed to bring cheers to the depths of December. Even the few skirmishes they had undertaken with the men of Cliffside, working alongside Gray, had proven successful enough to raise spirits. With Cecily recovering from her illness, and no further misfortune having befallen Long Ridge, they had decided to have the grandest of feasts they could in the circumstances. The women headed into town to gather what they could. The bastle itself was a beacon of light in the gloom, with candles lit at every window, and on every surface possible the glinting of polished metal, with all the family's pewter and silverware smartened for the occasion.

Meg sat at the table, stitching together garlands to decorate the main hall, whilst Hannah and Lizzie wove intricate designs from greenery: anything to brighten the room for as long as possible during the evening's party, as the men in the kitchen and local cottages prepared the meat for cooking. Everyone was more jovial than they had been for months, she thought, looking around at the happy little group.

Then there was Will.

Despite their stolen kisses, and their growing openness with each other, she still wasn't sure she could read him as well as she could the others. He was so good at switching from her charming handsome raider to just another of the young men of the village, boasting about their bravery: how they were sure they could take on the Grays and Elliots combined, and still come out victorious. She was certain she was more constant.

"More thread, my lady?" His words startled her.

"Will? Um, yes, thank you." She took the offered thread, and added it to her pile.

"I would like to meet with you, this evening, during the celebrations. I might just have a Christmas gift for you." Will grinned at her shyly.

"A gift? We didn't say we were exchanging gifts, did we?"

"No… I mean… You don't mind, do you? I could always give it to Hannah if you object?" The shyness had vanished, as his eyes sparkled.

"Judd might, even if I don't," Meg teased him. "But no, that will be perfectly acceptable. I'm sure I can find some trinket lying around that you might like. Somewhere." She made a show of looking through the sewing basket.

"I shall look forward to receiving my needle and thread then. After the last course is served, out in the barn?"

"No. Will, we cannot go creeping about the outbuildings in the middle of a party. Imagine what people might think. I'll be on the seat outside your sister's cottage. In plain sight."

"You don't trust me? Or you don't trust yourself?"

She batted him away. "Just go! I might see you this evening. Depending on the quality of your gift, I may permit you to dance with me."

He winked as he walked away, leaving Meg painfully aware that she was blushing. Desperate to avoid any questions, she left her work and retreated to her curtained chamber. Once alone, and calmer, she reached carefully under the thin mattress to retrieve the small package she had brought back from Hexham. Nobody had seen her slip the contents into her basket as the ladies had perused the blacksmith's wares, trying to find gifts for their menfolk on a limited budget. In the end, decorated pins had been purchased for her brothers, each with a carved image of a bastle-house at their end, a joint effort between blacksmith and carpenter.

For Will, though, Meg had chosen something different. She hadn't dared hope for a moment that he might have thought of her, but regardless, she had chosen a pin for him too, to keep his cloak close around him on colder rides. At the centre was a carved image, but one which she knew he would understand as referring to them and their relationship (such as it was), and theirs alone. A horse's head.

CHAPTER TWENTY

Long Ridge was practically shining, despite the early evening darkness setting in even more than usual, with the threat of rain hanging over the village. Everyone had made the effort to make their cottages look festive, and as Meg looked out of the window from her chamber, she could hear a mixture of singing and laughter rising up. Granted, it was tuneless and confused, but what did it matter, when everyone was able to have a good time and relax for a couple of days?

She saw Will, Cecily and Tom making their way over to the bastle, passing Ben as he headed out to the village perimeter. They may have been feeling festive, but they weren't being careless; a full watch rota had been established, to ensure they couldn't fall prey to any surprise attacks during their enjoyment. Meg hoped that even the Elliots celebrated Christmas.

The musicians had started in the main hall, crowded and bustling with almost all the village present, ready to relax and enjoy themselves. Meg watched as drink flowed, food was served, and ramshackle dancing began, informally at this stage, before the tables would be cleared away later allowing more space for moving around.

"It never gets dull, does it, the Christmas feast?" said Robert, leaning across to her.

"It's good that we've had sufficient fortune throughout the season; enough to enjoy it," Meg replied. "We all owe you and Judd a debt of gratitude. You and all the men."

"It's a good point," he replied, rising to his feet. "Everyone! Ladies and gentlemen, please, will you join me in a debt of thanks to every one of you who has taken part in a raid this last year, to enable us to eat and be merry this evening? It has been a hard year, but thankfully, we have made it through with no losses, and only minor injuries.

Even if one of them was to a non-raider, hey Will?"

Meg felt a rush as everyone in the room turned to look in Will's direction, laughing together as he blushed bright red, the same colour she was convinced she was turning. Even her ankle began to throb, as though in sympathy. She didn't dare look at him, but Robert wasn't stopping there.

"Will turned an almost-disaster into an opportunity to make himself indispensable around here, despite being a newcomer in Long Ridge terms. It appears he makes an excellent manservant, if any of you young women are looking for a potential husband for future consideration. I'll certainly look forward to him being around for a long time to come." Robert raised his cup in toast to Will, joined by everyone else, shouting his good health for the year ahead.

Meg had no choice than to join in, but found herself looking at the other women in the village, rather than Will, trying to assess whether they were looking at him as a potential husband, or even as a lover. She had never considered that anyone else would see him that way, assuming that she was the only one he teased, flirted with, and sought out time after time. What if there were others? What if he had a line of them, waiting one by one to meet him after the last food had been served, to see which gave him the best Christmas gift in return for whatever piece of frippery he had picked up in the market? Some of the others were indeed sitting a little straighter, fiddling with their hair, or untying and retying the cords at the waists of their dresses.

She chastised herself inwardly. What sort of woman was she, after all? Hadn't she said to Will herself that she was a sister to reivers, a reiver woman herself, one not to be messed with? What she was not was a silly girl who was going to let a young man turn her head, or let petty jealousies ruin what might be real. She slipped her hand into her pocket, felt the small slip of velvet she had found to wrap Will's gift in, and gripped it for strength. The other girls didn't have any connection with him, she was sure of that.

As soon as the last plates of food had been cleared, and the tables moved back to allow more space for dancing, Meg caught Will's eye across the room. Her plan to slip away was immediately foiled by the strong arm of Judd dropping around her shoulder.

"Come then, little sister. Now you are healed, we shall finally have the dance you have owed me since October," he shouted over the music, louder now, battling the conversation, and pulled her into the middle of the room.

"My beloved brother, once again taking on the duties I have never found to my liking," called Robert, raising his cup to them both.

***

At the other end of the room, Hannah stood with Will and Tom. "So which of you is going to ask me to join you?" She looked at them both, then held out her hand to Will. "I think you'll be the safest choice."

"Safest?"

"Well, we cannot have any other lassie wandering off with you, can we? I'm sure somebody special is waiting for the right moment to escape. Or am I very much mistaken?"

"I cannot think what you mean, but maybe it isn't safe for me after all – what will Judd think, if I'm seen to be dancing with his fine lady?" Will raised his eyebrows in challenge to her, but inside, he was starting to worry. Did Hannah suspect something of his feelings towards Meg?

"Pah, 'his fine lady' indeed. He's lucky if I look twice at him of an evening. Perhaps seeing me having the pick of the village's handsome young men will make him come up with a better gift for me than another cloth flower for my hair. Come on lad." She took Will's hand more firmly, and pulled him to join the growing group in the middle of the room.

Soon enough, everyone was dancing, giving Will the perfect moment to offer to swap partners with Judd, who happily took his lovely Hannah by the hand, slipping his arm around her waist as the music's tempo increased.

Will reached for Meg.

***

It was the first time since Will had stopped helping her around the village that he had really held her, Meg thought, as his hand moved to find a comfortable, natural resting place in the middle of her lower back. She hesitated for a heartbeat, then settled into the position, spinning around the room with him, neither them nor any of the other couples taking any formal steps, more a melée of movement, with formality thrown out of the window.

"This feels too daring," she whispered into his ear, as they found themselves on the outside of the group, almost in the corner of the room.

"Daring? We are surrounded by other people, and your brother himself just called out that the other women of the village should look to me as a husband. We are hidden in plain sight. Who would suspect a thing?"

"Are you looking to any of them?" The words were out of her mouth before she knew what she was saying. She felt him tense, saw his eyes darken.

"Why would you say that? Now, here, why?"

"I don't know. I… suppose… I worried."

The darkness faded, as a smile brightened his face. "You worried? Do you fear I'm about to abandon you? That I've been having clandestine meetings with others behind your back?"

His words were indeed what Meg had been fearing, even if she had only admitted it to herself minutes before, but the soft smile on Will's face suggested she had been anxious over nothing. "You're not, then?"

"No, it's only you. Whatever 'this' is, I have no clue,

but you're the one I have it with, I swear to you."

She felt herself relax at his words. "I'm not a silly girl, fawning over a petty jealousy," she said, to convince herself just as much as Will.

"I know. You're a strong, level-headed woman who knows her own mind, and knows how to act on it, who has just happened to fall for the handsome young raider who injured your ankle."

Laughing despite herself, she rested her head against his shoulder as they continued to dance, ever so slowly making their way to the door which covered the way out of the bastle, and into the fresh air.

CHAPTER TWENTY-ONE

The muffled music from the bastle gave the whole village a more jovial atmosphere, as Will and Meg made their way out through the enclosure and between the houses. They could just make out the lights from the four small torches carried by the watch, but not the men themselves.

"We still cannot go anywhere we might be thought to be acting suspiciously," said Meg, reaching for Will's arm, feeling braver now they had actually left the building.

"The smithy? We can say we thought we saw a spark, were just checking everything was well?"

Meg nodded. The small forge at Long Ridge didn't produce the intricate work of the smithy in Hexham, but their man was skilled when it came to shoeing horses or fixing wheels. The residual warmth from his forge would also be a welcome relief from the chill which was building as the night progressed.

"I do love that we live in such a trusting village," said Will, slipping through the unlocked door.

"Shush. I know some would say we have the right to wander in and out, but it's always felt wrong, taking advantage of our position," replied Meg, easing the door closed behind them. "No, the door should be open."

"Meg, please. I understand your concern, but I swear I'm not looking to do anything… untoward. Despite what others might say, it isn't all we think about. I mean, unless…"

"No! Will, no. I do have your Christmas gift though."

"And I yours."

"You first," she pushed him, keen to have time to rethink in case she deemed her gift unworthy in return.

Will paused for a second, then reaching into the pocket of his jacket. "I hope you like it," he said, placing a small parcel, wrapped in sackcloth and tied with red string, into the palm of her open hand.

Her fingers trembling, she pulled loose the knot, and gently unwrapped the cloth. There, in the middle of the parcel, sat a small box, carved from antler, with metalwork decoration.

"It's beautiful," she whispered, her fingers tracing the delicate pattern.

"Sweeting, the box is just the box – look inside."

Only just managing to unfasten the clasp, Meg did as instructed, and gasped. Inside, lay the most beautiful brooch she had ever seen. It was in the shape of the sun, with tendrils of silver representing its rays and set stones glistening against the metalwork.

"Oh, Will, it's, it's stunning. I can't believe it."

"It was my mother's. Cecily and I managed to get back to the cottage after the fire that… well… after the fire, and salvaged what we could before fleeing into the village in the next valley. Somehow, the strongbox had survived, with all her prized possessions still safe inside. Cecily always said I had to give it to somebody special, once I found them. Will you accept it?"

"It will be an honour, if you are sure," Meg replied, placing the box carefully on the table, before reaching for her gift to Will. "I hope you will feel the same about this, but it's nothing compared to that brooch." She handed over the velvet pouch, watching anxiously as he unwrapped it.

"Meg, it's perfect." He pulled her close, leaning down to her as their lips met.

Reaching her arms around Will's neck, Meg felt a rush inside her that she knew was getting harder to fight each time they touched. They had already been gone long enough for their absence to be noticed; somebody could come to find them at any moment. Breathless, she pulled away.

"Will, we can't. Not now."

"But soon?"

"But soon."

With a final kiss, she slipped out through the door, and back towards the bastle.

***

Will leaned back against the door of the cottage. He didn't want to go back; he didn't want to be amongst the hustle and bustle of the party for a while. He passed the horse-head pin back and forth between his fingers. She had gone out of her way to find something which meant something, which represented a little bit of what was somehow becoming 'their story'. The idea both terrified and intrigued him. He wasn't meant to be falling for her, and yet he had just gone and given her his own mother's brooch. It was all moving too fast, but not fast enough. He couldn't ask for her hand in marriage, not given his meagre offering as a potential husband. Robert and Judd likely had some grand plan for her, marrying her off to the son of a local merchant, or even a wealthy landowner; she was pretty enough, and had perfect manners to be able to fit in anywhere. Anywhere other than a cottage he shared with his sister and her husband.

Suddenly deflated, he pulled himself together and headed out to join Ben on the hillside.

"You don't think anyone really will come tonight, do you?" he asked, as he approached his friend.

Ben shook his head. "There's been no word, no rumour, and more importantly, no sign of any movement, but we'd be stupid to ignore the risk. And we made sure the word was out that we'd be doing it. We thought it best if everyone knew Long Ridge would be defended, even over Christmas. They think there's more of us out here than back at home, so we should be safe enough."

Will was glad to hear it. The idea of any harm befalling

Meg now sent shivers of fear through him. He must have been staring back towards the bastle for too long, as Ben broke into his thoughts.

"Missing somebody back there, are we?"

"Me? No, not at all, why would you think that?"

Ben barked out a laugh. "Because I've been making polite comments about the safety of the place this last while, and you've been looking towards the village as though you wish you were back there. Which, I might add, you might as well be, if you're going to be paying that little attention. The whole of Scotland could likely come through here and you wouldn't notice them."

"I'm sorry. It's just… I don't know. Perhaps somebody… Somebody who might be interested."

"Then go back to them, and have fun. You're not on the list for being out here, so why are you wasting your time talking to me? Go and show off those fine dancing feet, and tell my Lizzie I'm thinking of her."

Will didn't need telling twice.

CHAPTER TWENTY-TWO

Spring 1472

The longer, brighter days of an early spring led to the commencing of the raiding season in the borderlands, with news of attacks coming more frequently, as dwindling supplies forced hardened reivers as well as desperate farmers into theft to keep their families from starvation.

Meg and the women of Long Ridge found themselves back in the usual pattern of watching, waiting, and worrying, as their menfolk rode out every couple of weeks. It had always been bad enough, but now that the Mathers brothers had thrown their lot in with Gray, the women felt they had even more to be concerned about.

Gray was confident, more confident than a reiver of his class should have been. He was no Elliot, although his actions made it clear he thought he was. The daring nature of his raids over the border, or even amongst the English towns and villages, were becoming more and more feared across the Middle March, and Meg suspected it was only a matter of time before he began going even further afield. It wouldn't have been a problem, if the Long Ridge men weren't at risk of being carried along with him.

"Do you have to go?" she implored Robert one evening, as the men were about to ride out. "We have meat for the table, plenty of it, and our crops are growing strong. Tom said so just this morning. So why put yourself and others at risk?" Meg knew the answer, but felt the need to ask the question anyway.

"He's strong, Meg, and if we join him…"

"… we're seen to be strong too. I know, I do understand, but you're still paying the Elliots, so we're already protected."

"Protection from two quarters can only keep us safer

from trouble," Robert replied.

"Or at double the risk if the two of them fall out," Hannah muttered under her breath, but not quite quietly enough.

"They will not fall out," Robert snapped, turning his horse to face Hannah. "Gray is over-confident, I'll grant you that, but even he wouldn't have the nerve to tackle the Elliots. They're far too strong, even for the likes of him. So, we are safe." He nodded to the women, before leading the group out of the village.

The event, if not the conversation, was repeated time after time that spring. Meg tried to take comfort from their full barn, rising crops, and accounts book which had plenty more positives than negatives. For once, their clothing could be replaced rather than repaired, and she even treated herself and Hannah to new pins for their hair. Being able to take some momentary pride in their appearance was indeed a rare thing in their lives. But the money couldn't compensate for the fear. It wasn't just for her brothers and friends; now there was also Will.

If the men were treading a fine line between the Grays, Elliots and Wardens, she felt she was walking an even finer one, waiting with terror every time the group rode back into Long Ridge, worry coursing through her if he wasn't one of the first to dismount, letting her see that he was well. Meg watched in envy as Hannah and Lizzie greeted Judd and Ben in fond, relieved embraces, whilst all she could do was nod at Will, hoping her smile was enough to let him know she was thinking of him.

CHAPTER TWENTY-THREE

Summer 1472

"You've done what?" Meg didn't even try to hold back her anger.

"Meg, please, it needs to be done. These last three months have been some of our most successful. Surely you can see that?"

She hardly registered Robert's words. "But here? Why here? It's bad enough that we've had to work with him so closely this last season, but why must he come here? Do you really want Gray here, in our home, looking at our things? All he will be doing is working out what he can come back and steal on one of his next raids."

"Oh come, Meg, we have an agreement, he wouldn't—"

"You too, Judd? I thought you despised him as much as I do?"

Judd held up his hands in mock surrender, not helping improve his younger sister's mood.

"You're right, I don't like him. The man is too grasping by far, and willing to use the most awful of means. But, but," he said, pointing at her directly now, "you know how all this works. Now isn't the time to turn on him. And so yes, I agree with Robert, in that he and his entourage should be welcomed here to dine."

Meg slumped into a chair. "Well don't expect me to welcome him with my finest smile."

"I would like you to welcome Bridget," said Robert, kneeling in front of her.

"He's bringing his wife?"

"And his son, Henry. It will be a good chance to build relationships between our communities. Look, he's strong, and we could do with that, especially as the Elliots will be looking to build on their successes just as much as we are, following such a good spring. So please, for me, just be kind to Henry and Bridget, if nothing else?"

"You know I would always be kind," she said, reluctantly smiling at her brothers, glad to receive the same in return. But she could see that, like her own, those smiles didn't quite reach any of their eyes.

Knowledge of the Cliffside visit to Long Ridge had spread throughout the village before the end of the day, with most sharing Meg's sentiment of anger and nervousness. It was one thing to go out on a raid with somebody, knowing that everyone should, in theory, be working together for mutual success, but quite another to invite somebody with such a reputation into your own home.

"It isn't what I would have chosen, but Judd can be quite a charming convincer when he tries," said Hannah, as she and Meg perched on Meg's rocky ledge, looking out over the village below. Before Meg could reply, she continued. "I'm just going to say this, and I don't care what you say in return, but you and Will need to watch your step whilst our guests are present."

"What?"

"Don't play innocent; I know you too well for that by now, young lady. Don't think I've not noticed you and Will, playing your little games of attraction and resentment. Worst and best thing that ever happened to you, that stupid business with his horse, but whatever you might think about things, there's something deeper at play here, although I don't know what yet."

"Deeper how?" Meg suddenly didn't care that Hannah had suspected there was something between her and Will, but if there was something she needed to worry about, that was important.

"Haven't you noticed how he reacts whenever Gray is mentioned? You're so wound up in him, there's no chance you've not seen it. Honestly."

"No, I mean, something, perhaps, but I assumed it was just anxiety for the raids."

"Anxiety?" Hannah scoffed. "That young man is one of the bravest we have. No, it's something to do with Gray, but he won't tell me, however hard I try. You'd be best trying yourself. See if you can find out what's going on, in case it affects your brothers."

"Will would never do anything to endanger any of us. You know that."

"Not intentionally, but if there's something that happened in the past, then it could be that Robert and Judd need to know about it. Maybe Will hasn't thought of it that way." Hannah let the silence hang between them, as she began to play with the cord at the neck of her dress, holding the gown together.

"I should speak to him."

"You should. You should stop dallying around, pretending nothing's happening, and make sure that if there's anything important, you can pass it onto your brothers as soon as you're able."

"Come on then. I might as well go speak to him now, and get the deed done."

They found Will in the barn, checking that the animals were safe. They were lucky; those that had been lost through one raid had been replaced soon enough by another, and the Warden had had bigger issues to be dealing with than to investigate their relatively minor thefts. Hannah pushed Meg forward, not bothering to hide the fact that she was intending to wait and listen to the conversation which ensued.

"Everything well here?" Meg asked, tentatively, uncertain how to approach a potentially difficult subject with him, especially after recent events which meant she no longer knew for sure where she stood with him.

"As well as we can expect, I'd say." Will glanced

between the two women. "Can I help? Is all well with you?"

"It's, well, it's difficult, Will, but, well, it's about Alexander Gray." She watched for his reaction, suddenly aware of the sharpness in his eyes.

"What about him?"

"Well…" She didn't get any further.

"What aren't you telling us?" Hannah demanded, stepping around Meg to stand between her and Will. "There's something; I can tell there's something. And if it puts my Judd in any danger, then believe me, you will not want to meet me next."

Meg saw something like fear flash across Will's face as he opened his mouth, hesitated, then went to start again, but still nothing came. His hesitancy unnerved her for a moment, until she watched him compose himself.

"It's nothing like that. Or it shouldn't be. I don't know him, or at least I didn't, and he has no way of knowing who I am, but our paths crossed when I was younger. It was him, Meg, who led the raid on our village. He set the whole place ablaze when he found we had nothing left for him to steal. My… my parents… they didn't survive."

Without a moment's hesitation, Meg crossed the gap between them and threw her arms around Will, drawing him close. "I'm so sorry, Will, I'm so sorry."

Will looked up from Meg's embrace, at Hannah. "It wasn't a feud, it was just a raid, if that's what you're thinking. We were just unlucky." His eyes were beginning to fill with tears. "I hate him, if you want the truth. I wouldn't grieve if he didn't return from one of his raids, but I won't do anything to endanger any of our men. You have to know that. But please, please don't tell Robert and Judd."

"You poor boy. They won't hear anything from me, you have my word." With a gentle pat on Will's arm, Hannah left them without another word.

"It was him? He killed your parents?" Meg didn't

release him.

"It was just as I told you. Everything exactly as I said. I just… I just couldn't bring myself to let you know it had been him."

"But English on English?" It was just as the Warden had told them. If Gray had done it before, maybe it was he who had attacked Fourtracks, falling back into his old habits.

"A mistake, I'm sure. You know how things can be, out on raids. You can't tell north from south sometimes. But it's all behind me. I meant what I said," Will assured Meg, kissing her hair before pulling away. "I'm glad to see that you care."

"Of course I care, you idiot. That's why I'm so angry at you. Surely you can see that by now? I have to go and speak to Hannah, but I do care. Don't forget that." She reached for his hand, pulled him close, and kissed him gently on the cheek. "Be careful."

***

'Be careful.' The words were rushing around Will's mind like a bolted horse. It had been one hell of a day. First the news that Gray would be formally visiting Long Ridge, the home he and Cecily had felt so safe in, then revealing the truth of his past with the man, and finally, those words. 'Be careful.'

It was no declaration of love, yet somehow, it felt more important, more solid than if Meg had told him she wanted to run away with him. You only told people to be careful if you cared about them. So she did care. The Christmas gift had suggested it, and all the secret smiles, those stolen kisses, but he still wasn't sure just what her feelings for him were. Whether that was a good thing or not was something he would have to ponder over the coming days and weeks, but for now, there were preparations to work on for the Cliffside visit.

CHAPTER TWENTY-FOUR

Alexander's formal visit to Long Ridge was a blur of social niceties, far beyond that which the residents had bothered with before. Even when Wardens had passed through to discuss business with the brothers, they had never troubled themselves to go to such lengths. The second-fattest cow from the herd had been slaughtered, and the men gathered to talk business, as the senior women of the village sat around the fire talking amongst themselves. Bridget had brought no female companions, so sat with Meg, Hannah and Lizzie. The three main Long Ridge women tried to engage her in their friendly buzz of chatter, Meg doing her best to keep her promise to be kind.

Meg was only half-listening, trying to keep one ear on the conversation happening at the table on the raised dais. Will had found himself invited to participate, so she would no doubt get most information from him later, but it didn't feel enough. She wanted to be at the heart of things, to know what was being agreed, and to know whether or not she would be playing a part. She tried to read Robert and Judd's faces, to discover whether they were pleased or angered as to the direction talks were moving in, but they were too good for her. This was why she never gambled with them, she thought, a rare smile coming to mind. It had not been a day for smiling, since discovering what had happened to poor Will's parents. She wondered how he and Cecily could stand to be in the same room as the man, realising that by managing to be civil in front of such evil they were far better actors than she could ever be.

Finally the talk of raids and how to best continue their efforts ended, and the men left the table, beckoning to the women that food and drink were now in order. Meg rose, nodding to the young girls who had been brought in from the village to help her and Hannah, indicating that the food being prepared in the nearby cottages should be brought across. She hadn't wanted their bastle to look impoverished, feeling it gave a much better impression to appear that they had servants cooking their food elsewhere and bringing it over to them. Never mind that on every other day their food was cooked on the very fire she had just been sitting beside, doing nothing more useful than gossiping. It wasn't an image or notion which sat comfortably with her, but she knew that her brothers wanted to make a good impression on Alexander, his family and his men.

Tray after tray of food was brought in, as the men of each party gathered themselves along the trestles and benches which had been set up. Meat in various sauces, the best bread they could make, vegetable broths, and to accompany it all, their finest wine and ale was splashed into cups and distributed freely.

As the meal progressed, Meg kept a watch over it all from her place at the top table, trying to work out what sort of man Alexander was. She didn't want to look at him directly, but appraised him from the side, glancing along to him whenever she was sure his focus was elsewhere. He had dressed well for the visit, but then, so had everyone, she thought, checking that the agate on her necklace was still central to her neckline, and her silk-edged sleeves were straight. Alexander was all in black, with silver studs marking the seams of his doublet, shirt and breeches. Hats had mostly been abandoned by now, but Alexander had retained his jerkin and cape, both again covered in silver studs. Meg imagined he was trying to make himself appear bigger than Robert and Judd, who, whilst also predominantly in black and white, had both opted for blue doublets that day, the main colour of their family's badge.

In contrast to her husband, Bridget Gray seemed as though she was trying to disappear. Her dark red gown was almost brown, blending in with the wooden chair she was sitting in. Her dark hair was tinged with grey, despite her relative youth – she could only be Robert's age, after all – and her eyes looked dull through tiredness, however hard she tried to hide it, laughing at Alexander's increasingly cutting remarks. As for their son, Henry appeared to form a middle ground, neither making an impression, nor vanishing into nothing; he was just 'there', not making any impression on anyone. Meg didn't bother giving him a second thought.

Once the meal had been served, and Alexander's attention diverted with more discussion of raids and problems over the border, Meg reached across, tugging at Bridget's sleeve.

"Will you come for some air, my lady? I fear it will turn to hunting boasts soon, and we are better away."

Bridget's smile reached her eyes for the first time since she'd arrived, and she nodded. Only Judd and Robert glanced in their direction, as Meg, Bridget and Hannah slipped away to the upper floor of the bastle, and up to the roof.

It was a few minutes before any of them spoke, shawls held closely against the cool evening breeze.

"You're so lucky here, to have your brothers' protection," said Bridget. "They're good men, true."

Meg nodded, unsure how to respond. Hannah clearly had no such issue.

"Do you need a brother's protection then, dearie? There's always been plenty of space in their hearts for a damsel in need of saving. It's how I ended up here, after all."

"They saved you?"

"Aye. Well, Judd did, before Robert called him back to their father's home. I nearly fell prey to a monster of a man, who tried to make me his mistress in return for the life of my kin. Judd was a true friend to my cousin, was having none of it, and saved the pair of us. I like to think he was mostly interested in saving me so he could have me all to himself. Born the wrong side of the bedsheets was

Judd, but Robert doesn't mind. When he returned to the homestead, I was part of the package, as it were."

"And we're glad of it," said Meg, slipping her arm through her friend's. "But you," she looked at Bridget, "if you need our help, against anyone, or anything, you need only ask. We have plenty of friendship, more than enough to spare."

Bridget nodded, looking nervously at the door which granted access to the rooftop. The sound of male voices and laughter had increased in volume, and Meg suspected the other ladies had made themselves scarce by now. None of their little trio were keen to return just yet.

"It must be a challenge, being married to a man like Alexander," said Hannah, to Meg's surprise. "He seems very… active, shall we say. Rather full of character."

Bridget nodded, eyes downcast. "It can be difficult, when things go badly. But when things are good, he's very generous."

"I'm glad to hear it. As long as he looks after you." Hannah glanced at Meg. "We all need somebody to look after us, however hard we pretend we don't."

Bridget did not raise her eyes. "He's very generous," she repeated.

The door to the bastle's upper floor opened, and Lizzie's blonde head popped through. "Ah, I thought I might find you up here. I 'rescued' these, and thought it might do us all good. There's talk of your group heading home without sleeping, and I know I don't like a long journey without some warming fluid inside me." She handed Bridget the first cup of the four she had stacked inside one another, and pulled the stopper from the bottle she had precariously held tucked under her arm. Bridget took it with gratitude.

"The men of Cliffside aren't staying? I presumed we were providing accommodation for the evening? I hope nothing untoward has happened between the men?" Meg went immediately to the comment which could potentially be a catastrophe for Long Ridge.

"Untoward? No, not at all. A messenger arrived for Alexander, advising that a major raid is due to take place over towards the West March, and if Gloucester and his men are distracted enough, well, there is opportunity for the Cliffside men to take advantage of the slight gap in attention. They intend to return before first light, rest for the day, then move tomorrow night. According to accounts downstairs, it could be fruitful."

"Will our men be involved?" Hannah asked the question before Meg could open her mouth.

"No, not this time; Alexander is going for this one alone," Lizzie replied. "It needs a greater understanding of the area than Robert and Judd have, and he doesn't want to be slowed down."

Meg felt herself relax. Their men would be safe this evening, and no hint of their connection could be traced back if anything went wrong.

In silence, they gladly drank the offered wine, and looked out across the darkness of the night.

CHAPTER TWENTY-FIVE

"What did you think of young Henry, then?" asked Robert the next morning as they broke their fast. As Lizzie had reported, the Cliffside group had set off just after midnight, keen to make the most of the possible advantage at the western fringes of their territory.

"Well, he's young, you're right about that," replied Meg, risking a glance at Will to see whether he knew where this conversation might be leading. He shook his head, out of Robert's line of sight.

"Not too young," replied Robert.

"Not too young for what?"

"Marriage."

Meg spluttered. Crumbs caught in her throat as she began to choke on pieces of bread, on air, on what she feared her brother was suggesting. "Not for me?" she practically squeaked.

"Well obviously for you – Judd won't give up the lovely Hannah, and I can't go offering the maidens of the village these days, can I, like some ancient tyrant? Their menfolk would object, and none of us would want that." He chuckled at his words, then stopped when he noticed his sister wasn't joining in.

Meg caught Will's glance as she caught her breath. "But, you never said anything," she managed, in a hoarse whisper.

"I wanted to see you together. We both did, Gray and me. He's in agreement, it seems an excellent match."

"An excellent match for you two perhaps, but not for me!" Meg exclaimed. "He is little more than a child, what, sixteen years old? A whole five years younger than me! And completely undermined by his father on all counts. You must have seen the way they were together? Alexander is a monster, a bully, and his son is completed cowed. And besides, apart from civil greetings, I hardly spoke to him. You couldn't possibly have seen how we were together to make such a judgement on whether we are remotely suited for each other."

Meg could hear the mix of anger and panic rising in her voice, not caring whether her brother could hear it too. Henry Gray was not the man she intended to marry – even if there were no other options presently available to her, that her brothers would readily agree to.

"I cannot marry somebody who appears to have no voice, no thought of his own. You must see that?" Despite the residual ache in her ankle from the forced merriment and activity of the night before, she rose and rushed out of the room, leaving her brother and Will with eyes wide.

Reaching her own space at the top of the bastle, Meg threw herself down onto the bed, burying her face in the thin pillows. Marriage? To young Henry? A permanent tie to Alexander Gray and Cliffside? That was not what she had seen in her future. She was no fool; she knew she would marry – it was what was expected. She would marry, settle down, and run a safe, secure household for her husband and the family which would follow. Only, in her head, that household had always been Long Ridge. Robert had shown no sign of taking a wife; he had never even shown interest in any woman save for a few brief affairs, none of which had lasted beyond a few weeks, sometimes even just days. Meg had seen her destiny as being to find a husband, and to stay at Long Ridge, managing the bastle and village, with Robert somehow handing things over to her husband as he grew older, unable to lead the raids as he always had done. Judd would marry Hannah, eventually, and the five of them would muddle on through, side-by-side, keeping one another safe, with her sons being raised to carry things on long after they were all departed.

For a moment, she wondered whether Henry could still fit into that plan, moving to Long Ridge with her, but that moment swiftly passed. She had seen Alexander and his son together; there was no way that man would ever let his son out of his control. She would be moved to Cliffside, and potentially never see Long Ridge or her brothers again.

At least there would be Bridget, she mused, realising her pillow was becoming wet with tears. Another surrogate mother figure, combined with an elder sister, just as Hannah had become. But again, with what purpose? Meg suspected Alexander kept just as tight a rein on his wife as he did his son. And could a home really have two mistresses, even if one was as ineffective as Bridget appeared to be? Meg surely wouldn't be given the freedom she currently had at Long Ridge.

A noise behind her distracted her from her thoughts. In that moment, she didn't know who she most wanted to see: Robert, to berate him for such a monstrous idea, or Will, to comfort her in her hour of need.

It was neither.

Judd stood just inside the curtain, with an expression on his face that she so rarely saw in him: uncertainty. He was always so sure of himself, of his decisions, of everything. Whether it turned out right or wrong, Judd knew it was for a reason, and whatever decision he made at any time was the right one for that moment. Whereas Robert was cautious, Judd believed in following his heart. They were a good working team.

At this moment, though, he didn't look himself.

"I heard," he said, without preamble, sitting himself on the edge of her bed.

She sat up, leaning into him, as he enveloped her with a strong hug.

"No, that's not fair. I knew. I knew before, I mean. Robert told me what he was thinking."

She tried to pull away, but his grip was too strong.

"I know, it feels like treason, but how could we tell you? You wouldn't have been yourself, and we wanted to see you both naturally, to see whether there was any affinity."

"Then you will have seen that there was not. How could there have been, when the boy doesn't seem to have a thought of his own, or a tongue to express it even if he did?"

"But you don't hate him?"

"How would I know? He was devoid of any character. So no, I suppose I don't hate him, but neither do I like him. I 'nothing' him, because there is nothing of him to form an opinion of. Surely you saw that as much as I did?"

Judd nodded. "I am sorry, lass. I know he's not what you want, but you do see the need?"

"Of course I do, but with you and Hannah, and Robert on his own, I just assumed that when I married, we would stay here. It's not the idea of marriage I hate, I'm no fool, it's leaving Long Ridge. It's my home, and I hoped it always would be. And there's Will."

She had said his name before she realised what she was doing. Why was he suddenly featuring in her future plans? This was not what she intended, and especially not in front of her brother.

At the mention of Will's name, Judd pulled his arm away, moving to crouch in front of her, their eyes level.

"Will? What has he to do with this? Have you and he…?" His voice trailed away at the end of his question, but she was in no doubt as to what he was asking her.

"No! Of course not. Nothing has happened. I don't… I don't know why I mentioned his name. He's nothing, nothing whatsoever." She knew she was rambling, but couldn't help herself.

Judd narrowed his eyes. "You must be telling the truth now, Meg. Trust me, whatever you might be thinking about this young man, you must never look at him in that way again. You must be utterly chaste and committed to whatever marriage Robert agrees for you. Do you hear me?"

Meg nodded. It wasn't enough.

"I said, do you hear me?"

"I hear you. But there is nothing to agree. There is nothing between Will and me other than one, single, mistaken kiss. That went no further, and I do not intend to let it. That has been agreed by both of us." As the lies tripped off her tongue, she decided that mentioning the other 'mistaken kisses' would not benefit either of them.

"Good, I'm glad to hear it. Marriage is not to be toyed with, not when a man like Alexander is involved. I wouldn't see it as a sensible action to take a lover when you're married to his son."

"You think I would be interested in Will as a lover? Please, acknowledge me as having some sense." She hoped her face wouldn't betray her, given that was exactly what she found herself wondering about. More than she would care to admit.

"I know you've plenty of sense in that head of yours, lass. I just wanted to hear it all for myself. Well, look, I'll leave you to it, but please, just, speak to your brother. Let him know you understand. That it will be alright." He rose, and mussed her hair with his hand, always his sign that he loved her.

She smiled up at him, but knew it would take more than a conversation of brotherly love to convince her that she could even be slightly content with marriage to Henry Gray.

CHAPTER TWENTY-SIX

It took another hour for Meg to compose herself sufficiently to return to the main room of the bastle. She wasn't content with Robert's plan for her, whatever Judd might try to convince her, but she knew that Robert wasn't actively choosing for her to be miserable. She had seen the way Alexander acted the night before, with a confidence about him that he would get his way, regardless of anyone else's opinions. Yes, he might give the impression that he was taking their thoughts into account, listening to other options proposed, but he certainly wouldn't abide by them, not unless it suited him. Somehow, his plan, his way forward, would always be the best, would always be the one which went ahead.

Meg supposed that's what made strong leaders stronger. And yet, Robert had always managed to balance it: taking on board the thoughts of his men (and women), combining them with his own to come up with something of mutual benefit. He knew their lands better than anyone, but he also knew the strengths of his men. Perhaps Alexander did too, and his men didn't have such strong wills at those of Long Ridge.

Robert was still at the table, as though he had been waiting for her to return. He had surrounded himself with documents, but maps this time, and was leaning over them, tracing routes with his finger.

"A new raid?" Meg approached him slowly.

"Possibly an old one. But done afresh. Just a couple of miles over the border. I'm worried that we shouldn't leave it too long before going back out. It's been long enough since our last raid, and that was with Cliffside. I don't want people to think we are becoming vulnerable."

"Why would they?"

Robert sat back in his chair. "It's a strange thing,

aligning ourselves with somebody like Alexander. He's a strong man, feared and admired around here, so nobody from our side of the border will touch him or his property. So, by working alongside him, we share that strength, we gain some element of protection, with people knowing that by hurting us, they could anger him, and face a degree of retribution. On the other hand…" He shifted in his seat. "On the other hand, if we're seen to be relying on Alexander, then it makes us look weak, and an easy target, potentially, for anyone who thinks we need the men of Cliffside to bolster our own position."

Meg was glad of the change in topic, not wanting to discuss what was currently hanging between them.

"But we aren't weak, and we know that. So by undertaking a raid of our own, whilst Alexander and his men are occupied elsewhere, over to the west, we demonstrate that we are working with them for mutual gain, not because we need to?"

A smile spread across her brother's face. "Exactly. See, one day, you'll be managing all this for yourself, and you will be just brilliant at it."

The reference to her future brought Meg's happiness crashing down around her. "Managing all this for myself? Where, exactly?" She regretted the words as soon as they left her mouth.

"Ah, come now lass, you knew this was coming one day," Robert said, standing and moving around to where she stood. "Just give the idea some time, please? See how things are after a couple of days. Nobody is going to whisk you away to Cliffside in the dead of night, against your will, alright? You have my word."

Meg looked up at him, knowing that although that might be true, she still didn't have long until she was going to be leaving her beloved Long Ridge. The thought of this almost caused the tears to flow, but she resolutely forced them back down. She would not show weakness, not in this moment. Nodding, she turned her attention back to the map on the table.

"So, what is the plan?"

Clearly sensing that the conversation was closed for now, Robert gestured for them to sit down, and they began to discuss the finer detail.

CHAPTER TWENTY-SEVEN

That night, once silence had fallen across the bastle, Meg crept from her bed and down to the enclosure, silently slipping through the well-oiled door of the bastle's lowest floor. To her relief, Will had got her message, hurriedly written and slipped into the saddle of his horse as she pretended to check on them earlier. It was a blessing that her former servant was regular in his habits, always taking the chance to take Patience out for a ride.

There he was, waiting for her, slipping out of the shadows just as she approached, his eyes glinting in the moonlight. Meg glanced around, checking that they wouldn't be seen, but she knew her fellow villagers: if they had the chance to be warm in their beds on a night like this, cool despite the season, that's exactly where they would be. Exactly where she would be, if she had the choice, and being given permission to be sharing it with the man of her choice. She put such thoughts out of her mind; it wasn't as though she had a man in mind, was it? Seeing Will's familiar shape coming out of the shadows jolted her for a moment. 'One mistaken kiss' – that's how she had described it to Judd – but now she couldn't help wondering if there was more behind it. Regardless of her feelings, it was Will she wanted to talk to at this moment. She needed to tell him exactly what her brothers had planned for her, and find out his thoughts on the matter.

He narrowed his eyes at her as they both sat on the low bench on the outside wall of the bastle, tucked out of view of anyone other than the most diligent of guardsmen, and frankly, they had all known her long enough for her to know that none of them would have given her away if seen.

"Well? Did you get out of it?" His questions came out more rushed than Meg would have expected.

She shook her head, surprised to find his arm suddenly around her shoulders, pulling her close.

"I'm sorry."

"For what? Not as though you care." Meg knew she sounded petulant, but she didn't have the strength to do anything about it. She needed his reassurance, that was all.

Silence.

"Do you?"

"What?"

"Do you care?"

"About you marrying Henry? What do you think?"

Meg slumped against him, unsure of whether she was glad or disappointed by his reaction. Would it have been better if he had rushed upstairs, sword in hand, demanding her brothers leave Meg to choose her own husband, and that in his opinion, the only suitable man would be him?

"I have to leave. We have to leave." She said it quickly, as though getting the words out and into the world would make the decision easier, perhaps even convince him to leave with her. As though by saying it slowly would in some way allow her brain to catch up with her heart, and remind her what she was saying, and how ridiculous it sounded when any sense of logic was applied.

"Leave? To where? And 'we'? What 'we'?" Will replied, his voice sounding confused.

"We have to leave Long Ridge. Both of us. I cannot go alone, what chance would a woman have on her own out there? You have to come with me. Not tonight, but not too much longer. Within the week. Within days if we can. Gather what you can, and we can meet, like this, and run away. We could go over the border. We could set up home, somewhere quiet. We could marry. I'm sure in time, you would get used to the idea." Even in the darkness, she could see the confusion on his face at her words.

"Run away? Us? Meg, you've gone mad. I cannot run away with you; your brothers would kill me. Alexander would kill me. He might even kill you."

"I'd rather be killed than marry Henry Gray."

"No, no you wouldn't. And I won't do it. I won't bring ruin on you and your family, not after they've been so good to me. Not because of that monster. He won't destroy another family I care about."

"Then what?" Meg had pulled away from him now, escaping the protection of his arm.

"This is all just a shock reaction because of what happened this morning. You don't actually want to run away with me." Despite his effort, she could tell there was a hint of a question in his words.

"I might. How do you know what I'm thinking anyway?" she hissed, furious at him now for not following what she had seen as such a sensible line of thought. "If we run, there's nothing to be done about it. We will be gone, and that is that. My brothers, Alexander, Henry, they will all have to accept it."

"Do you really think that if this is what Alexander wants, he won't seek retribution on anyone who tries to bring about an alternative? Anyone who dashes his plans? And who do you think he will seek such revenge on?"

"He will likely go on some ridiculously daring raids to prove his manhood, and, if we are lucky, find himself thrown from that beast of his, and break his neck."

Will sighed. "Think, Meg. He will come storming over here, his men at his heels, and likely kill anyone he finds. But it won't be us, not if we've run. It will be your brothers, Hannah, Ben, Lizzie, everyone. He won't spare a soul. I know, remember? I've seen it, from both sides."

Meg turned away and leaned against the stone wall of the enclosure, before glancing up at the darkened windows of the bastle. Of course, Will was right. Alexander was not a man to be messed around. The dullness of Bridget and painful shyness of Henry were testament to that.

"I don't want to leave Long Ridge," she whispered, turning again and burying her head in Will's shoulder.

He wrapped his arms around her, and kissed the top of

her head. A tiny piece of her heart broke.

CHAPTER TWENTY-EIGHT

She couldn't bring herself to speak to Robert again the following morning, but by the middle of the day, Meg had summoned the courage she needed, and sought out her brother. She found him in the barn with Judd, checking the state of the animals which had survived the winter. Despite the brightness of the sun, the wind was keeping the temperature down, and she pulled her shawl close around her as she entered the shelter of the building.

"I'll do it," she said, forcing as much confidence into her voice as she could, keeping her tone steady. She couldn't bear for them to hear her falter.

Judd half-smiled at her, as Robert closed the gap between them and embraced her tightly.

"It will all be well, little sister, I promise you. You'll always have the protection of Long Ridge behind you, you know that."

Judd nodded in agreement. "If Gray steps out of line for a single moment, you get word to us, and we'll be with you in a heartbeat."

"I doubt Henry would have the courage to step out of line, but thank you with regard to Alexander," Meg replied, a slight shudder at the thought of the man who was to become her father-in-law. "At least there will be Bridget. She is a good woman, despite her mousey nature, and I suspect she will be kind to me. I think she would enjoy having a daughter of sorts."

Not having the strength to discuss the matter further, Meg removed herself from Robert's arms, and left without another word.

She couldn't watch when Ben left the village that afternoon, knowing that in his pack he carried a letter from Robert to Alexander, formally acknowledging that the proposed marriage was to go ahead, with no cause for delay. Despite being significantly younger than Meg, Henry at sixteen was perfectly able to give his consent, and with Meg having just turned twenty-one, there was no cause for the marriage to be put off.

The touch of a hand on her arm distracted her.

"I reckon you'll have a month, my dear, then you'll be ready for the off," said Hannah, watching Ben vanish over the horizon.

"Just a month?" Meg found her eyes drifting down to the enclosure, as Will was tending to Patience. "It isn't long enough."

"For what?"

"Never mind." With a half-smile to her dearest friend, Meg turned away from the window. One month to prepare herself for marriage didn't feel anywhere near long enough. Quite apart from the mental strength she would need to find from somewhere, Hannah had provided her with a list of items she needed to take with her, to furnish a marriage home.

The lady in question appeared again, as Meg consulted the list, her entire wardrobe spread across her bed.

"I'm going to be living with Alexander and Bridget for at least a few years before Henry and I have our own home to manage. Do I really need so much?" she asked.

"I assume, dearie, that you're doing this to take your mind off the fact that Ben will have delivered your brothers' message in a matter of hours?"

"You should never assume anything, Hannah; it muddles things," Meg retorted. "But yes." She dropped heavily onto the chair next to the bed. "How can I do otherwise? The marriage is happening, whether I like it or not, so all I can do is ensure that I am prepared. I know the men would argue the opposite, but let us be open here, my friend: it is I who shall be the wiser partner in this coupling."

Hannah raised an eyebrow.

"Not like that! You know I don't mean like that!"

"Your handsome young warrior hasn't stirred your passions then?"

Meg threw a shawl at Hannah, indignation clear across her face. "He certainly has not! How dare you say such things?" Any hint of a smile was gone.

"It was in jest, Meg, that's all, a jest."

"Well, it isn't funny. There has never been anything untoward in my and Will's relationship, nothing at all. And it won't help me in my travels to Cliffside if rumours to the contrary are heard being spread from within my own home." Tears began to prick at Meg's eyes, but she was determined not to let them flow. She rose and turned away from Hannah, giving herself the chance to rub them dry.

"I'm sorry. I've not said anything beyond these walls. You know I wouldn't."

Meg sighed, and sank down again. Without another word, Hannah moved to join her, wrapping her arm around Meg's shoulders. "It'll all be well, you'll see."

"I'm sorry, Hannah," said Meg, resting her head on her friend's shoulder.

"It's forgotten."

Meg sighed an internal sigh of relief. If anyone caught a hint of how things truly were developing between herself and her handsome raider, there would be hell to pay.

CHAPTER TWENTY-NINE

The bastle had a sense of calm to it those next few weeks, the warmth of the summer causing life to gradually return to something like a normal rhythm for the residents of Long Ridge. With the exception of Meg. She wasn't sure what 'normal' would even begin to look like when she was wed to Henry, and in the meantime, what was the use in feeling settled into a home she wouldn't be able to call such for much longer? At least Will provided some joy for her: an odd combination of hope and excitement, with their snatched kisses and embraces when certain that nobody was around to witness the act. It went no further, but not for lack of wanting – certainly not on her part, and from the way his body reacted during their illicit encounters, not on Will's either. But she had to wait; they both knew that they couldn't let it go any further. The risks of discovery were too great for both of them.

The arrival of the object of Meg's thoughts distracted her from her memories of their last meeting. That had been the most risky and tempting so far, the way his hands had explored her body, coaxing her gently to do the same with his. She flushed at the thought of it, feeling the heat rise. How could he look so casual, when she felt the eyes of the whole village on her?

"Well met, Mistress Meg!" he called, raising a hand in greeting.

She nodded, and was torn between glaring at him or scuttling off, when something else caught her attention. Growing up in a border village, everyone's senses were acutely aware of when something wasn't quite right. A lone rider was skirting the horizon, just visible below the ridge, in shadow against the sun behind.

Meg glanced at Will, knowing he would have followed her gaze. With an almost imperceptible nod, he headed into the bastle to fetch Judd and Robert. By the time all three men had joined Meg back in the enclosure, the rider was dismounting.

Hal, Alexander's right-hand-man at Cliffside, was known to them all by now. His gruff manner belied his good sense, giving the wrong impression he was no better than the muscles and bulk which were obvious to all.

"Mathers," he addressed all three siblings collectively, not bothering to waste time on such niceties as first names. "Bad news from Cliffside."

For half a heartbeat, Meg found herself hoping it was the nulling of the marriage agreement binding her to Henry. Her eyes and thoughts had again drifted to Will, when common sense reminded her that such news would most likely arrive by letter, not be delivered in person by Alexander's second-in-command. Something then, bigger?

Robert nodded to the man to continue.

Hal paused for a moment, as though the effort of a full sentence might prove too much, then took a deep breath.

"Bridget is dead."

For a while, none of them said a word. Longer than was appropriate, Meg was starting to think, until Will stepped forward.

"I'm sorry to hear your news, friend. Bridget was a good, kind woman. Come, I'm sure the brothers and Meg would wish me find you refreshment whilst they compose a message in response."

Stunned at the sudden formality of his words, Meg could do little more than nod as Will escorted their now-guest into the bastle.

"She's dead," she said, dully, once they were out of hearing. "How can she be dead? She was here. She was well."

"I don't like this," muttered Judd. "Too convenient, too neat."

Robert nodded. "Meg, stay close to us. Under no circumstances allow yourself to be alone until Hal has left the village. Do you understand?"

"Alone? But…? What, you imagine he is here to kidnap me?"

"Or ruin you," said Judd, his face dark. "We've no idea where Alexander's mind will take him or his men. If you're thought to be without virtue, the wedding will be cancelled."

"He could use this as an excuse to overrun us all," added Robert.

"He has just lost his wife," Meg protested. "And my virtue is beyond reproach, I thank you to remember." Something she was now even more grateful for, if it was likely to be an issue.

In the following silence, she could sense her brothers were thinking about poor Bridget, just as Meg was. The woman had likely never harmed a soul in her life.

"How did she die, I wonder?" Meg asked out loud.

Robert squared his shoulders. "Let's go and ask Hal."

CHAPTER THIRTY

"She fell?" As much as he was clearly trying to disguise it, the disbelief in Robert's voice was evident to all.

Hal looked ahead defiantly, as though he had expected such a response. Apparently poor Bridget had fallen down the outside steps of the bastle during the night, losing her footing in the darkness, and breaking her neck as she landed.

Judd continued. "She had lived in bastles like Cliffside all her life. She knew her way around her own home. And what was she even doing going out on the external steps at that time?"

"We don't know the full circumstances that led to the incident, only that the tragedy befell her two nights gone, and that the terrible accident has been reported. She shall be buried as soon as possible."

"We will, of course, send a representative to the funeral, to pay our respects to the lady who would have become kin by marriage," said Robert, his dark eyes glancing at Meg, who responded with an almost invisible shake of her head. "Ben and Lizzie shall attend, on our behalf. We have much to do here, and cannot leave the village without an armed presence now that the good weather is returning. I'm sure your master will understand that."

Hal nodded. "Aye, sir. We already hear word of Scots coming south over the border, attacking the more northern villages, taking what they can. Retributions have already started too, though, and we formed part of a hot trod ourselves just two days before this sadness befell us."

"We had heard of raids beginning again, but had hoped they would not reach us yet," said Robert, the concern clear in his voice. "It seems we must be ready for a full advance."

"If it please you, I will return. But my master noted that he would be in touch soon, regarding wedding preparations." Hal gave them a half-smile, and began to gather himself to leave.

"Surely there will be a delay to the wedding, as Cliffside will be in mourning?" Meg found herself saying, clutching to the thin strand of hope which appeared before her.

"Nay, mistress, we will be needing a wedding to bring us all through our sadness. Gray was very particular about that." With a nod, Hal departed. Will escorted him back to his horse, returning a few minutes later, to find the siblings had not moved.

"Do you believe she fell?" Meg demanded of the three men who now surrounded her. "Bridget Gray? A weak woman, perhaps, God rest her soul, but not a stupid one. This death is no accident. I can feel it."

"Have a care, Meg. If you continue thus, then you're either accusing either Bridget of suicide (and condemning her soul), or accusing somebody else of murder, and that brings with it far too many dangers." Judd glanced around them. "I know we four would not let that rumour leave this room, but you mustn't say anything beyond these walls."

"Have no fear, Judd; I shall be careful. But you must have your doubts?"

Robert broke into the conversation. "Whatever our doubts, we will not speak them out loud. Personally, I find it unbelievable a woman of such experience and good sense would be wandering around the outside steps of a bastle in the middle of the night, and without decent boots on her feet. But if that is what Gray has told us, then I'm afraid that's what we must accept. But not necessarily believe."

Alone with Will, perched on the rock where they had had their first blazing argument, Meg pushed him to say what he thought.

"I'm with you," he said, drawing in the ground with the tip of his sword. "A woman like Bridget doesn't fall. But nor do I believe she would throw her soul into damnation by jumping."

"Leaving murder," Meg whispered.

"Leaving murder," Will agreed. "Look, I know this is difficult, and I know I have no claim on you, that I never can have – but I want you to be careful when you leave here."

"Ah, my young warrior, you're a traitor to your type, going around admitting care for people. It might be love next." She nudged him gently, but kept her eyes focused on his.

"Do not mock me, Meg. You're… you're special, and you know that. Just promise me, will you?"

She placed her hand on his knee, gently squeezing to acknowledge his request. Then, hearing footsteps approaching, she planted a fleeting kiss on his cheek and moved away.

CHAPTER THIRTY-ONE

When Ben failed to return after a second night, and with no word received from Cliffside, Robert sent Will and two other men after him, concerned that something had happened between the two villages. As the sun set that evening, a clattering of hooves alerted everyone to the group's return.

Meg caught Will's attention as he entered the bastle's main hall. An almost imperceptible shake of his head warned her against approaching him. Instead they went directly to Robert and Judd, who were leaning against the wall by the fire, talking.

"Sirs, there is news. Gray accepted your condolences with ill grace; he is angered by rumours."

"Rumours?" asked Robert, alert now.

"There is gossip. We heard it as we stopped in a village on the way; the tavern was full of it. The rumour is that Bridget's death was not an accident." Ben studiously did not look at Meg, but she felt the eyes of her brothers on her, and moved to join the discussion.

"They claim it was Alexander?"

"Nobody dares say his name out loud in connection to it," Ben replied. "But it's there, beneath the surface, and it's obvious enough who everyone suspects."

"We must ensure we do not add our voices to any gossip," said Robert. "Will, Ben, I want you to go now, to every house in the village, and make this very clear. The official word from Long Ridge is that we send our deepest sympathies to our neighbour, and soon-to-be kin, on his sad loss. Is that understood?"

The two young men nodded, and made their way out to go about their instructions.

The mood at Long Ridge did not improve over the

next week, with travellers coming and going, and rumours getting wilder with each telling. The men and women of the village did their best not to be dragged into the talk, but when accusations of Alexander Gray throwing Bridget from the roof of their bastle reached Robert's ears, enough was enough.

"This has got to stop now!" he roared at the gathered villagers the following Sunday, after the priest had departed, leaving the floor of the church to Robert. "We cannot afford to be pulled into this. Whatever our personal opinions or thoughts may be, we cannot afford to anger Gray over this incident. The next time you hear a hint of the rumour passing the lips of anyone within this village, you must send them directly to me, is that clear?"

The murmured agreement was not what Meg was expecting, but it seemed to satisfy her brother, for now at least.

Another message from Hal that same evening changed everything.

CHAPTER THIRTY-TWO

Meg stood, stunned into silence, as Robert and Judd shut the trapdoor which separated their private chambers on the bastle's upper floor from the hall below. With the three of them alone, she still couldn't find the words to fill the void between them. Her brothers appeared to feel the same: Judd sank onto the nearest chair as Robert dropped onto his bed. All the dividing curtains were pulled back.

Eventually she found her voice.

"He cannot do this. Can he?" The latter was added with uncertainty. She was starting to think there was nothing that Alexander Gray couldn't do, if it suited him.

"There's no real reason why not," Robert replied.

"Other than basic decency," snapped Judd.

The letter from Alexander still lay on the table in the middle of the room. The letter stating that, given the circumstances, and the youth of his son Henry, the most sensible course of action for all concerned was that Meg should marry Alexander, not Henry, and become the mistress of Cliffside. Of course, the note had conceded, there would need to be a suitable time of mourning. Therefore the marriage, which had been due to take place in less than two weeks, would now be delayed until a three-month period had elapsed.

"Three months to mourn his wife, and then replace her?" said Meg, skimming the note again, half-hoping she had missed something, some tiny hint of a reprieve from the horror which was starting to flood through her.

"I've known men take a wife quicker," said Robert.

"But after something like this?" Meg demanded.

Robert shook his head. "No, I suppose not. Usually after loss through illness."

"Exactly, illness. Where the end is expected. Or even through old age. We know marriages around here are as political as any other, and that a lovely new bride can be waiting in the shadows, to move up to the position of wife when an older woman dies. But this? Bridget was no aging or ill wife. She was causing her husband no embarrassment. She was doing nothing against him at all."

"I think that's the point, sister: she was doing nothing." Judd's voice was quiet. "I think he perhaps sought new adventures, so to speak, and possibly couldn't stand the idea of his son having something more appealing than him."

"I am to be a trophy, to be won and displayed? Nothing more than a prize cow, and no better when it comes to breeding, I'm sure. He wants another child, is that it?"

Judd shrugged, and fell silent again.

Robert filled the emptiness. "I will speak to the priest, but as you are only promised to Henry in word – no ceremony, and certainly no consummation – I cannot see any true reason why he cannot do this."

"And I suppose my being entirely opposed to it does not count?" Meg cried.

"Meg, at least this way you are warned. You know what you are going into. He could just as easily have got you over there, and on the very morning of the wedding switched places with his son, giving you no chance to be prepared."

Meg shook her head. "He cannot do this," she whispered again, as much to herself as to her brothers. "Please?" she implored them.

"We cannot risk it, Meg. I am so sorry. But look on it this way: you will be mistress of the whole village, just as you are here, in charge of all decisions, the home, the bastle—" Judd didn't get the chance to finish his sentence.

"In charge? With Alexander Gray as a husband? I doubt very much that I shall even be in charge of what I wear each day. You have to do something. Is he so powerful that even the wonderful Mathers brothers can do nothing against this? What are you not telling me?"

The brothers looked at each other, with Judd nodding to Robert.

"What?"

"There have been other rumours. At least one man, overheard to accuse Gray of the murder, has been found dead at the side of the road. Where all would find him. Stabbed, bled to death, a nasty way to go. Whoever did it was careful. There's not quite enough evidence to prove Gray and his thugs were responsible, but it was at the edge of Cliffside's land, and the victim had been particularly vocal."

"The man is a monster," Meg breathed. "And he is to be my husband. I need to get out of here." Throwing the letter back onto the table, she pulled open the hatch and descended to the floor below. She ignored Hal, but beckoned to Will to follow her.

"I need to exercise my horse," she said, to anyone who was listening. "Will shall accompany me."

It took her three attempts to tell Will why the tears had begun to flow the moment they were out of sight of the village. He was stunned into the same silence as she had been, before pulling away from the embrace he had wrapped her in, as soon as her eyes had filled.

"Will, what? What is it? You cannot agree with this, surely?" Meg rubbed her face with the long sleeves of her dress.

"Agree? What, no, of course not, but have you gone mad? We must return, now, before we are gone too long and it is remarked on."

"But why? What are you talking about?"

"Can you not see? We are alone! You are unchaperoned! If we didn't risk Gray's anger by running away when your marriage to Henry was announced, how can we be so stupid to be alone now? If word gets back…" He was already back on his horse, bringing hers around by the reins, signalling for her to mount. "Be sure that your gown is exactly as it was. There can be no hint of anything untoward."

"There has been nothing untoward. A friendly embrace. Between friends."

"You know we are more than that."

"Nobody else does."

Will shook his head. "It won't matter, not if the rumours start. And look at what has already happened to one who spoke out against Gray. I'll not risk that fate for either of us. You mean the world to me, Meg, but I won't willingly lose my life out of stupidity. Come, back to the village."

He spurred Patience into action without another glance at her, leaving Meg fighting the frantic thoughts in her mind. She had inadvertently put them both in danger, but equally, she meant the world to Will. He had said it.

Despite herself, as she followed him back to the track, she found something to smile about.

CHAPTER THIRTY-THREE

Frustratingly, on her arrival back at the village, it seemed Will had been right; Hannah's clicking of her tongue proved that.

"What were you thinking? You cannot just go off with other men now you're betrothed."

"I wasn't 'off with other men' – I was out for a ride with a trusted member of my brothers' household. One who was put in direct charge of my care not so long ago, by those very same brothers. As you well know," retorted Meg, whilst checking that Hal was out of earshot. "He must have seen us leave anyway."

"Ben had some sense, and rode after you, saying he would join you both, as he had the urge to go out himself."

"I didn't see him," said Meg, only now noticing Ben tying up his horse in the enclosure, only feet away from Patience. The two men were deep in conversation, Will's face dark with worry.

"That's of no matter. At least he says he was with you, and as you and Will arrived back together, the worst of it is past. But you cannot do that again. Not now. It was one thing when betrothed to that young stripling who wouldn't have a clue what was what, but quite another now that your intended is his father. You watch your footing from now on, you hear me?"

"I am tired of being warned of things," said Meg, as they entered the main hall, and sat at the table. "Is this how life shall be from now on? A constant string of warnings about how to behave, how not to upset my husband?"

"You listen to me, Margaret," said Hannah, suddenly holding Meg by the shoulders. "This is not the life we would have chosen for you, but tragically, this is the life you find yourself dealt. These warnings are not given out of anything other than love for you, and a care to see you navigate the months ahead with ease, in the hope that you might find some semblance of happiness. Robert is even now drafting the letter which will tie you to this man, knowing that he doesn't want to do it, but that there is currently no alternative. I have been so lucky to find the man I love, and who loves me, and I wish you could have had the same fate. But for now, this is your lot. Please, do everything you can to make it go as easily for you as possible."

Seeing the look in Hannah's eyes, Meg chose not to argue, but simply nodded her agreement.

Only once Hal had left, the note to Alexander safely in his pack, did Meg dare seek out Will again, finding him in what had become their spot rather than hers: the large rock at the end of the village.

"He's gone then?"

She nodded, sitting beside him. "And so it is done. A couple of months, and I shall be the 'lady of Cliffside', not that such a title will bestow any semblance of power. I'll be little more than a trophy to him, just as he prizes his latest cattle capture." She rested her head on his shoulder, in no mood for passion, rather for the comfort of his arms.

"Perhaps you'll be the woman to change him, and bring him under your spell as you've done with the men here."

"Spell? Oh, come, Will, don't start throwing phrases like that about, or he'll likely name me a witch." She smiled at him.

"Fine, not spell. Just be yourself. Be good at what you do. I've heard the tales about the time after your father died, where you practically ran the bastle and village. Even ordered raids for a period. Isn't that true?"

Meg grinned, her spirit temporarily restored. "Judd and Robert were lost. Didn't have a clue, completely buried in their grief. Don't think I didn't mourn our father – he was a wonderful man – but we needed to move on. We were at risk of being overrun by neighbouring villages. We could have lost everything."

"So you rallied?"

"I had to."

"Well, don't you think you have to again, now?" Will squeezed her shoulders, an encouraging hint in his voice.

"The stakes feel higher this time, somehow. That man, he sends shivers through me. With Henry, that would have been an easy enough situation to deal with. Once we were in a position to leave, or when Gray himself died, we could have taken on our own home and been in charge of our own destiny. But Alexander, it's a whole different circumstance. And he has surely killed his wife!" The latter was a cry. "How has the world shifted in such a way that he is not being punished for that?"

"Talk is that Bridget had no family left, or none which would be able to avenge her against Gray. She was all alone. He was all she had: him and their son. And can you see Henry doing anything against his own father?"

Meg shook her head. "I'm stepping into a dead woman's shoes, taking her place at the table, in her home." She shuddered. "In her bed. It doesn't feel safe. And yet, my brothers have agreed. How can they not see what they're sending me to? That is what hurts, that they are choosing this life for me."

"I don't think there's any way out of it, not without incurring the wrath of Gray and his men. Even with the Elliots' protection, it wouldn't be enough. I've been on a raid with them; they are barbarians, ruthless. The men they've killed or maimed in the name of spoils…" Will's voice trailed away for a moment. "Nobody is spared at their hand."

"I forget you have all witnessed it, even Judd and Robert. And so it must be done. I will marry him, but know that I won't forget you, William."

"I should hope not," Will replied, pulling her face close

to his, and claiming it with a kiss.

CHAPTER THIRTY-FOUR

Ben's return the next day confirmed everything Meg had expected: three months of mourning, and then she would be away to Cliffside, to take the place so recently vacated by Bridget Gray.

Sitting alone on the stone bench, she turned the paper over and over again in her hands, looking for a clue of sorts, as to whether Alexander Gray was, deep-down, an essentially good person, that all the rumours of violence and cruelty were just rumours, and that actually her married life would not be as bad as she was dreading. There was no comfort to be found. The note had been a cursory response, stating the date on which the postponed wedding would be held, and that his son Henry had given his blessing to the proposed union. She doubted that the latter was true.

There was a half-hearted attempt to cheer her by hosting a feast that night in the bastle, but all it did was remind her how much she loved Long Ridge, and the people she would miss when she was eventually forced to leave. This was the end of her dream of living out her days in her beloved family home. There was even a chance, however cruel, that Henry Gray himself could become master of Long Ridge; Meg would ultimately inherit the place if Robert and Judd both died childless. Meg hated that idea. She would have to have a word with Hannah, and try to convince her that at least one of their menfolk needed to get on with that most pressing requirement of any landowner: to provide an heir. She was sure Hannah would happily marry Judd, despite their current contented state of unmarried bliss. She knew the local priest had lectured them on more than one occasion about living in sin, and the need to marry and have children.

At the thought of her future nieces and nephews, Meg's

hand instinctively went to her own stomach. Would she end up giving Gray another child? Maybe it was the most sensible way forward; if she was pregnant, Alexander would have to leave her alone for at least a few months, once the child had quickened. Meg wondered if he would take a mistress. Or even mistresses. It wasn't unheard of, and the presence of Judd in their home proved that even their wonderful father had done so. As a wife, she was sure she should be against such an arrangement, but perhaps, if Gray found somebody else, she truly could just be the mistress of Cliffside in name, and let another take on the more unsavoury elements of the role. She did want a child, but once one, or ideally two, had been born, maybe that could be an end to things.

"But what about Bridget?" she whispered to herself. Bridget had provided Gray with a child, then outlived her usefulness to him, and look at what had happened to her. It must have been murder. And if he killed one wife, what on earth was to stop him killing another?

A chill ran down her spine, as she envisaged a tragic future. Her only choice, in reality, was to go to Cliffside, and be the best wife possible to Alexander Gray and keep him as happy as she could.

The thought did not warm her.

CHAPTER THIRTY-FIVE

Will couldn't focus. Six times in a row now, he had been beaten by either Ben or Tom, as the three men practised their sword skills out in the enclosure.

"Come on, Will, you're better than this," taunted Tom, as he once again broke through his brother-in-law's defensive position, bringing his sword down to where it could easily have broken Will's arm in a true fight.

Will just shook his head. "I'm not myself today. Not sure why."

"I think we know why," said Ben, stepping up to fight Tom. "You've hardly been eating, you're fighting like one of the bairns with a wooden sword, and if I catch you staring off into the hills one more time…"

"You'll what, exactly?"

Ben laughed. "It's a woman. It must be a woman. Which of the charming lasses has caught your eye? One of our own, or one from further afield? You keep watching the road, so maybe somebody you met in Hexham?"

Will opened his mouth to argue, then realised it was as good an excuse as any. "Yes, fine, from Hexham. Louisa, something. Didn't stop to catch her full name." He attempted a grin, in the hope it would satisfy their curiosity.

Tom waited until Ben had wandered to their kit pile to retrieve a different weapon, before approaching Will. "Louisa?" he asked, raising an eyebrow.

"Don't. Just don't. Please?" He glanced over at Ben, keen for Tom's doubting not to be overheard.

Tom smiled slowly. "It is Meg then?"

It wasn't worth arguing. "Always. But the fewer people who know, the better. Wouldn't you agree?"

The older man nodded, clapping Will on the back as Ben returned. "Your secret's safe with me, lad."

"Secrets?" Ben asked.

"Ah, not for your hearing, laddie. This is between brothers, of sorts." With another wink at Will, Tom raised his sword to begin the fight.

***

From their vantage point above the fake battles, Meg looked on. She too had been spending plenty of time watching the road out of the village, hoping, as she was assuming Will was, that there would be yet another messenger from Cliffside, bringing news of another tragedy. Of course it was wrong to wish misfortune to another soul, but would many mourn the loss of Alexander Gray?

Robert's voice startled her from her thoughts. "I don't want us to part enemies, Meg."

"We won't, Robert. We couldn't."

He put an arm around her shoulders. "He scares me. Not in a monster sort of way, more in a 'not sure he's aware he has a limit' way. I know he respects me and Judd to a point, and he's serious about us joining forces. We just need to work this the best way we know how – diplomatically."

"There's nobody in the borders can do diplomatic better than you. Look, Robert, I'm not happy about going, I'm never going to be, but there's no choice – I do see that. I'll make the best of it, for you. But I swear, you cannot abandon me to that place without promising me some relief now and then. I need a reason to come here, or for you to come to me. Please? You must at least do that for me?" She turned to face him, knowing her brother would never be able to lie to her directly.

"I swear. I won't just throw you to the savage and leave you to your fate."

"You never know, maybe Gloucester will best him, if he's keeping to the west for a while?"

Robert grinned. "It wouldn't be the worst news, would it? But let's focus on the plans, and at least keep you busy." He reached into the pocket of his jacket. "I wanted you to have this."

Meg eyed the long thin parcel carefully, before opening it. A dagger glistened in the sunlight streaming through the window.

"I mean, it's mainly decorative, of course. Not sure whether the blade could withstand even carving meat, to be honest with you. But know that you'll always have our protection, if you should need it. I'm sure Ben or Will would fly across the valleys at a single word."

At his casual mention of Will, Meg held her breath, but as her brother continued, she saw it was just that: casual. "We'll have to see about the pair of them marrying soon. Lizzie will be anxious for Ben to do the decent thing, I'm sure, but I don't know about Will. Do you?"

"Me? No, not a thing." Meg hugged her secret knowledge to herself as Robert smiled at her, kissed her forehead, then returned to his work on the table.

CHAPTER THIRTY-SIX

The next messenger, bringing news from Cliffside, tore through Meg's heart.

All hopes of the freedom she had wished for were dashed. Permission had been granted for the wedding to go ahead, all talk of betrothal to Henry forgotten, and the local priest advised of the change in situation. According to reports which crept into the village later that same day he hadn't been overly keen, but Gray had persuaded him that in view of the strange circumstances it was the more sensible course of action.

Gray's decree that only two of Long Ridge's men need accompany Meg was the part which sunk her soul even further into despair. She had fostered almost fanciful dreams of having the ability to ride between Cliffside and Long Ridge, to see Will and her brothers, before returning each night to her new home. It was all that kept her going. And now this: just two men from Long Ridge to join her, and to link the villages. She was suddenly unwilling to sit and listen to the plans Robert, Judd and Hannah were making for her.

Half-blinded by sorrow and anger, it wasn't until she knocked on the small wooden door that Meg even realised she had reached Cecily's cottage. But it was Will who opened the door. Her Will. The one who had helped her so much this last few months. Surely he could help her now?

His faced darkening at the sight of her tears, Will pulled her towards him without a word, wrapping his arms around her. She responded instinctively, not caring in that moment that they were still in the open doorway, visible to anyone who might be walking past. A heartbeat later, they were in the main room of the cottage, Will kicking the door shut behind them and releasing her only to lift her face to his. Despite the tears flowing down her cheeks, she lost herself in the moment, drifting away in the comfort of Will's embrace.

A crash outside startled Meg halfway to her senses, and she glanced around the room. Will read the question in her eyes.

"They're not here. Won't be back until tomorrow. Visiting."

It was all she needed to hear, as she reached for Will again, and they pushed through to the cottage's inner chamber.

Light was fading when they stirred. Meg was first to wake, reaching instinctively for the woollen blanket which had tumbled to the floor, suddenly shy and nervous around the man who had formed such a key part of her life for so many months. Carefully, she moved to the edge of the bed, pulling the rough linen gown over her head, and tying the front as best she could in the half-darkness. One advantage the likes of her had over the gentry, she thought, smirking: she didn't need any help getting back into her dress.

"Will," she whispered, nudging him awake. "Will, come on, please."

With a half-smile, his eyes flickered open, as he tried to pull her back towards him, but she was too quick for him, leaning down to pull on her stout shoes.

"I have to go. But I swear, this is not over." She forced into her voice a courage which she did not feel, hoping he would be too tired and content to hear the cracks she swore would be obvious.

"Stay. Please?" He pushed himself up on one elbow.

Meg cupped his face with her hand, before leaning down to kiss him. With every fibre of her soul, she wanted to lie back down, to spend the whole night in his arms, but she had already risked too much, in every way. The familiar, heavy sense of dread threatened to overwhelm her as she began to realise what she, what they, had just done. But she forced it aside.

"I love you, you know that?" The words were said before she had even finished thinking them.

"It's a good thing, really, given that I love you too," Will replied, reluctantly nodding for her to turn so he could retie her laces. "More than anything."

With a final kiss, Meg fled.

As Meg stumbled back to the bastle, she was convinced the eyes of the village were on her. Judging her. Had she really just given herself so boldly to her young raider? Her heart burned at the thought of it, and she smiled to herself, despite the turmoil. All that talk of not allowing herself to be found alone with a man, and now this.

She pulled up short at the sight of her brothers and Hannah sitting together on what Meg was starting to see as 'her' bench. Would they be able to tell her secret? Would Hannah? She knew full well that her brother's relationship was far from platonic. Brushing imaginary creases from her skirts, she held her head high, and greeted them.

"Where did you get to?" Robert demanded, as she drew nearer.

"Up to my rock, that's all. I just wanted to be away from everything," Meg replied, hoping nobody had actually gone looking for her during her absence.

Her brothers didn't look as convinced as she would have liked them to, but a call from one of the men to go and check the barn was all the distraction Meg needed. With nothing more than a questioning glance, they rose and left the enclosure. Now she only had Hannah to deal with. Her friend was eying her with a curiosity Meg wasn't comfortable with.

"You look different," Hannah began. "And I doubt you've been anywhere near the end of the village."

"Nothing happened," said Meg, raising her chin to look as determined as she could.

Hannah's eyes narrowed. "I doubt that as well, but if you're telling me it was nothing, then that's what I have to believe, isn't it? But you be careful, young lady. Be very careful indeed."

"Nothing happened," repeated Meg, before walking past her would-be interrogator, and escaping to the relative privacy of her curtained chamber in the upper bastle. Her mind was racing, thinking and over-thinking about what she had just done. Sleep was not going to come easily.

CHAPTER THIRTY-SEVEN

A week later, tired from a series of restless nights, and more than one secret visit with Will, Meg was trailing in Hannah's wake, laden with baskets, and wishing they had taken her brothers' offer of a larger escort. The ride down to Hexham had been safe enough, with the market-day bustle giving everyone a sense of safety, but the men could at least have helped carry things.

Pausing by one of the stalls, her eye was caught by a huge mirror, far grander than her tiny handpiece. Suddenly, a reflection in the glass startled her. Gray? What was he doing here? Was he having them followed, now that the wedding plans were moving apace? Could he possibly have found out what happened the previous day?

He gestured to his retinue to pause as he crossed the street to greet them both.

"Ladies, a pleasure to see you. I do hope you are not here alone?"

"Good day," Meg replied, forcing a smile into her voice. "Yes, it is just the two of us today. We wanted to look at material, now that I am in need of new gowns, with less than a month until we are married. We saw no need for an escort."

She saw his eyes narrow for a moment. "Then I would consider it my honour, and duty, to send some of my own men back to Long Ridge with you. The roads can be a dangerous place on market day, you must know that?"

"We encountered no problems getting here, but thank you, Sir, for the kind offer. We shall of course take it, and with gratitude," said Hannah, placing a gentle but firm arm around Meg's shoulders.

"Yes, it's very kind of you," agreed Meg, easing herself away from Hannah's grasp.

"We heard you had been over at the West Marches,"

Hannah was continuing, apparently ignoring the flash of surprise in Alexander's eyes. Why wouldn't the Long Ridge residents know what their new allies were up to, after all?
"Yes, we have been exploring to the west a little more than usual, since Gloucester has been having issues with his Scottish counterpart. Let them keep themselves busy, and we can make the most of the situation. I'm sure Robert and Judd would agree."
"They likely would. It's a sound strategy, after all," agreed Meg, keen to show that both women were as up to date as the men when it came to planning.
Alexander smiled. "Well, we shall not keep you any longer. I also have matters to see to in town. These men will stay with you, and accompany you home when you are ready to leave. I will not have the March saying I do not look after my future wife." With a nod to them both, he was gone.
Meg smiled at the two men assigned to her and Hannah. They were smarter than the men of Long Ridge, that had to be admitted, and their weapons seemed in better condition. No wonder Gray always got his way, if his men were so well turned-out, even for a trip to the market. "We don't have much more to do, and we'll be on our way. You will be welcome to stay at Long Ridge, if you would rather not ride straight home."
The older of the two looked surprised at her offer. "That's very kind of ye, Miss. We might just do that. But you take your time, we ain't in no rush, we'll just follow on behind ye."
Despite the friendly nature of their new companions, Hannah and Meg didn't linger in Hexham any longer than required, selecting some new material, along with some fresh vegetables for their evening meal, and loading the men with filled baskets before returning to their small horse and cart, stabled briefly on the town's outskirts. Gray's warning seemed to ring true, as they encountered tales of theft and assault on the road earlier that day. Hannah didn't seem to notice, as Meg had, their escort's

keenness to get away from the rumourmongers, both ensuring their faces were covered until they were all on the quieter track to Long Ridge.

With two of Alexander's men present, having taken advantage of the offer of bed and board for the night, Meg didn't dare risk meeting with Will that evening. But lying in her bed, she smiled to herself at the thought of her handsome raider. The times they were able to find themselves together were limited, but they were certainly making good use of the chances they did get.

The next morning, Meg was regretting her decision to ride in the cart, rather than on horseback, from Hexham, as her stomach rebelled against the tiniest morsel of food she tried to force down. She was unable to face even her usual favourite treat of an apple, fresh from the market.

"Sunday," she mused to herself, realising the day, and counting back the weeks. Her courses were due to begin within a few days; that would half-explain it too. Making her excuses for not going to church, she retreated to her bed and didn't move for the rest of the day.

Ten days later, now battling the strangest urge to nibble on dry oats, and still with no sign of bleeding, Meg was running out of excuses for the sudden and strange changes in her choices at mealtimes. As she dealt with her own laundry, there was nobody to notice that the expected bleed hadn't arrived, but she had to accept that she was now mainly lying to herself. Gathering some coins, and the best bread and ale from their stores, she slipped out to the far end of the village. The cottage, well away from everyone else's, was still showing signs of life as she knocked on the door, hoping nobody had seen her.

An hour later she returned to the bastle, her suspicions confirmed. It was late June now, so with her last bleed in mid-May, the old woman had suggested Meg would be giving birth in mid to late February. At least the promise of more fresh bread had bought her silence, but Meg's heart felt anything but quiet, especially with the knowledge that there was now a second heartbeat echoing her own.

She had to get to Will.

CHAPTER THIRTY-EIGHT

"Pregnant?" Will repeated his question for the tenth time since she had found him, and dragged him to the seclusion of the stables, under the pretext of checking on Patience's hooves.

"Yes, Will, pregnant." Meg paced the front of the stables, away from the horses, even more determined to avoid another incident this time. She knew she had to stay calm, and think things through clearly, however strong the instinct to jump on the nearest saddled horse and run for the border. She suspected a hoard of Scots would be less terrifying that dealing with Alexander and her brothers if this particular piece of information was to come out.

"Will you… do anything with it?" Will asked, gently.

"I can't destroy a life, if that's what you're thinking. Old Annie asked me the same question, and offered to help if I wanted it. But I said no, and swore her to secrecy about the whole thing. It's our child, Will. We just need to keep our heads and be sensible."

"What do you mean?"

"I marry in what, two weeks now? We say nothing, I go to Cliffside, wait a month, and declare myself pregnant by Alexander."

She watched his face darken at her suggestion.

"Meg, no, I can't let you do that."

"What other option is there? I haven't had long to think about it, but going through everything I could think of, it's the only idea I could come up with which didn't end in the certainty of Alexander Gray trying to massacre everyone at Long Ridge." She tried to make it sound like a joke, but she knew there was nothing to laugh about. "Will you do it? Will you go along with my plan?" she whispered to him.

"Meg, I'm no expert, but the child will come too early,

you can see that?"

"Babies arrive early," she started to protest.

"But they're small when they do. Ours – yours – will be a healthy size."

"No, it will be just right," she assured him. "Think on it, Will. Gray's always keen to show off how brave and strong he is…"

The look on Will's face showed Meg that he had followed her line of thought. "He is so big and strong that even a bairn of his born two months too soon would look as though it was full term."

"Conceived on the wedding night too, no less," she added. "And what man would argue against him? Would you risk suggesting his lovely new bride had taken a lover?"

"You're going to have to be careful, you know that? On the night, I mean?"

She silenced any more of his worries with a kiss. "We'll sort it all out. I know we will. But are you happy, Will, for us? You're going to be a father."

He returned her kiss. "I'll make you both proud of me. I promise you that."

Meg hadn't thought she would spend the eve of her wedding watching out for the arrival of her future husband, with the feeling of a lead weight sinking through her stomach. She should be excited, happy, or at least broadly content. Instead, terror flooded her veins, and she could hardly hear a word Hannah, Lizzie, Cecily and the others were saying. They had gathered in Cecily's home, with the other women of the village, Tom and Will having been banished for the night as the married women gave their advice to Meg. The irony, she thought, as her mind drifted to the new life she and Will had created. The last thing she needed from her friends now was how to handle the wedding night. At least, not in that way. What she needed was advice on how to handle the temper of the man who would be riding into their village at any moment, who she knew could flash into anger at almost anything, and who she was so sure had killed his first wife. Other than resorting to poison, she wasn't sure there was much the women of Long Ridge could help her with there.

By the time the Cliffside men did arrive, she was beside herself, sick with nerves, and wishing she was able to confide in somebody other than Will why she was looking so unhappy when Alexander dropped from his horse to greet her.

Henry Gray, Meg realised, was looking as sullen as she was feeling, but at least he had a reason he could share with the outside world. Using nerves as her excuse, she escaped to her bed as early as she could, dreading what the morning would bring.

CHAPTER THIRTY-NINE

The morning of their wedding day was frustratingly perfect. Meg had hoped for rain, thunder, the greatest storm they had ever encountered, but no. The sun greeted her and Hannah as they woke, setting the tone of the day for all but Meg herself.

Meg dressed in silence, in a gown of bright, bold red. She certainly felt it suited the tone of the day, sacrificing the rest of her life for what Robert had kept calling "the greater opportunity", but it now felt as though he was trying to convince himself as much as anyone else. Her feet dragged on the way across the main hall, so slowly she almost tripped down the steps as she descended, immediately clutching her stomach as she regained her balance.

Out in the enclosure, she shielded her eyes against the mocking sun. She thought about digging her heels in, but knew it was pointless.

At the chapel entrance, everything stopped the moment her brother took her hand. This was meant to be a joyous occasion, filled with celebration, yet she felt she was entering her own funeral. The clamminess of her brother's palm told her that he was as nervous as she was. In that instant, they were children again, Robert and Judd sword-fighting with sticks, utterly engaged, until Meg had got in the way and found herself on the ground, tearless with the shock. Both boys had rushed to her, Judd's eyes full of guilt, but Robert offering his hand to pull her up. She had stood, determined not to show the pain in her jolted back. She would save her tears for her bed, when she was alone.

Robert squeezed her hand, bringing Meg back to the present. She smiled at him, as best she could. He had been there for her as a child; he would be there for her now if she needed him. And as she had been brave then, she could be brave now. Tears might come later, but in this moment, she needed as much courage as her raiding brothers had. She took a deep breath, and stepped forward.

But as she began to walk, Meg had to fight the urge to scream. To shout at the top of her voice that this wasn't fair, that it wasn't what she wanted, that it surely wasn't what any of them truly wanted, apart from Alexander. The already-close walls of Long Ridge's tiny chapel were threatening now, the comfort of childhood memories banished. She didn't let her eyes wander to the family vault, to the father she was sure would never have let this happen, or the mother who would have soothed her through it if it could not be avoided.

At the front of the church waited the man who represented her travesty of a future. For all their differences, all the arguments, she would have given anything to be walking towards Will today. She glanced at him, briefly, done up in his finest midnight blue velvet for the occasion. Part of the pile had been pushed the wrong way, Meg spotted, as she drew level with him and Cecily. She fought the urge to brush it back into place. That would not go down well in front of her future husband.

The incense was stifling as Alexander finally reached for her hand, casting an appraising eye over her attire. She returned the act, observing that once again he had opted for the silver-studded black. After all, he and Henry were, officially, still in mourning. It made the wedding even more of a mockery.

***

An hour later it was done, and they all returned to the bastle for the wedding feast, before the journey to Cliffside. Will watched Meg, impressed at her deception; the only difference in her demeanour was her limited choice of food. Although he could tell her smile was false, nobody other than Hannah and the Mathers brothers would have seen it. He wondered if they had, and were just pretending not to notice. Was that for Meg's sake, he wondered, or their own?

"Not drinking, Will?" Ben was at his elbow, holding out a spare cup of wine, full to the brim.

Will shook his head.

"More for me then!" Ben emptied the first, before talking a gulp from the second.

"You should be careful," Will scolded his friend. "You'll need your wits about you for the ride."

"It's two hour's ride, three at most. Meg's a strong rider. We'll be there before nightfall. Plenty of time for… well, for what's needed."

Will nodded, but turned away; that was not a topic he wanted to discuss. Despite his best efforts, it had pained him to see Meg up there, pledging herself to that monster. She hadn't seen what Alexander was capable of. He was willing to bet none of them had. But Will knew better. Will had seen it for himself.

Without warning, the memories of what had happened that night flooded through the walls in Will's mind that he had so carefully built up over the years. The cruel face leering down from the huge horse, the orange of the fire against the black of the night; it had become almost more of a painting than a recollection. But it was all true, and there was only one man at the heart of it. And here he was, about to do it all over again.

Will wanted to race up to the top table, to tear the new gold ring from Meg's finger, and tell them all what sort of man she had just married. But he couldn't. Meg wasn't his to win back. He could never offer himself as an alternative, despite their child – and if he disgraced her now, she'd never find another husband.

He was distracted by the sound of the musicians beginning to start playing in the corner of the room. Mostly Long Ridge men, they knew what their favourite girl enjoyed dancing to, and started with one of her usual choices. Will watched, clenching his fists so tightly that he almost drew blood from his own palms, as Gray claimed his new bride for the first dance. He had to bide his time; there was no point ruining anything.

***

Meg felt Alexander's arm snake around her waist, and held herself still inside to prevent the shudder in her mind spreading to her body. She couldn't risk giving him the slightest inclination that she wasn't divinely happy to have been joined in holy matrimony to him. Until death parted them. There was the shudder again. Soon it would be more than his arms she would be dealing with.

She moved through the steps, her feet feeling like blocks of lead, forcing themselves through each action. The thought of Will's arms wrapped around her wasn't helping her state of mind, and her stomach was full of fluttering wings. Her only hope was for the musicians to literally change their tune, end the piece early and move on to something else. A quick glance from their favourite local lass was enough, and the tempo of the tune lifted.

She fought the urge to sigh, as Alexander loosened his grip, leading Meg to her brothers. Robert half-rose, before Judd stopped him.

"No, brother – let the youngsters have their fun. Will? I'm sure you can do a better job than either of us could."

The young couple dared the swiftest of glances at each other before moving to the centre of the hall.

"May I have the honour, my lady?" Will bowed with formality.

"You may, good sir, if my husband permits?" Meg turned to Alexander, keen to show him, and the world, what a good, obedient wife she could be.

To her relief, he nodded, raising his newly-refreshed cup of wine in a toast to the pair.

The tune wasn't a romantic one; Meg wasn't sure she could cope with that, but it required enough contact to give her the excuse to wrap her arms around Will's neck on more than one occasion.

"If they increase the speed again, we're going to have to stop," Will whispered into her ear.

"No, no you mustn't."

"I'm not going to start throwing you around the room, my love, not in your condition."

She paused for a moment too long, before Will spun her into his arms again. "Careful."

"You don't think they can tell?"

"Sweetheart, even I cannot tell, and I've seen you in a lot less than you're currently wearing." He was whispering into her ear again, and she felt the heat rising in her cheeks.

"Come on, I think I should sit down a while," she said, taking his hand. "Or perhaps one of your admirers would like your company. Temporarily, of course." She nodded to the group of young women standing, looking hopefully at her man. "Go on – think of your reputation."

He grinned at her, his face lighting up, as he turned and made a show of picking the prettiest of the other girls for the remainder of the dancing, as Meg battled the nerves which were racing inside her, anticipating the night which lay ahead.

CHAPTER FORTY

However hard Meg tried to keep the conversations flowing once the dancing had stopped, eventually the moment she had been dreading arrived, as Alexander announced it was time for them to leave. After all, her trunk and bags had been packed for the best part of a week, with the final few items being thrown in that morning, as she finished preparing for the wedding.

Instinctively, her eyes drifted towards Will, as she thought of the brooch she had placed so carefully amongst her things. She had not quite had the courage to wear it to the wedding itself, for fear one of her brothers would see it, and know it to be a gift, but not from either of them. Once at Cliffside, she planned to wear it every single day, to bring her luck, and, she hoped, bravery to see things through.

But all that was ahead of her. For now, she had a two- or three-hour ride to get through, having already been on her feet for the majority of the day. Selfishly, Meg hoped that her new husband wouldn't quite have the energy to do his duty, but she had a feeling that Alexander wouldn't allow anything which might be considered a potential slight to his masculinity and power. Besides, she reasoned with herself, the sooner the act was done, the sooner she would be able to announce her pregnancy. She knew that men often left their wives alone during pregnancy, which was certainly an appealing prospect. In addition, the sooner the better if she was to stand any chance of convincing Alexander that the child was his.

As Cliffside came into view, she knew she was being ridiculous, trying to find differences immediately, when the bastles, and indeed the villages, of Cliffside and Long Ridge were so similar. Cliffside was slightly larger, if she was honest, but the square tower of the bastle looked just as strong as her own beloved Long Ridge, behind the low stone wall of the enclosure. The cluster of cottages surrounding it gave an element of protection to both.

"You're impressed? You should be. We've not lost anything more than a couple of cattle from the fields in the years since I took over from my father," said Alexander, a proud smile spreading across his face. "You'll be safe enough here. Safer than at Long Ridge, I assure you."

If only he hadn't added that last part.

"I have never felt anything other than safe at Long Ridge, I'll thank you," Meg snapped back before she could stop herself.

The smile vanished. "Then you've been a fool, I'm afraid. Long Ridge is nothing compared to this. Bigger, stronger, and richer. You'll be glad of the day you became its mistress, if you can learn to hold your tongue."

She forced her face into a smile. "I'm sorry, husband. It was not meant as an insult, just a statement of fact. But you are correct, of course, stronger is always better." The complement worked, partially. Taking her cue, Meg continued. "I hope you can show me around, demonstrate those strengths?" That completed it.

"I would be glad to, of course. And we can discuss your role in all of this, now you are lady of the house."

"My aim is to please, and to keep everything just as it ought to be," she replied, hating the simpering weakness she could hear in her own voice. Robert, Judd or Will would have pulled her up for such a sycophantic attitude, but Alexander seemed to revel in it. She made a mental note to be careful in her opinions now she was to call Cliffside 'home' – a strong-minded woman was unlikely to be a popular one.

As they stabled their horses, she deliberately focused on not looking where Will was tying up Patience's reins. She didn't dare notice anything about him now, she thought, as she let Alexander take her own reins and guide her to the other end of the building.

"Where are these two staying then, Sir?" Hal, Alexander's second-in-command, seemed to read Meg's mind, shoving his thumb at Ben and Will.

"The old forge at the end of the village; might as well be used for something," Alexander replied, practically sneering as the two young men were directed to the small building, the furthest from the bastle.

"They will be provided for within the bastle, I understood was the arrangement?" Meg asked, smiling at Ben, not at Will.

"Yes, yes, as was agreed, I'm sure. Quite why you need an escort is beyond me."

"Sir, we are not here as an escort for Mistress Gray, we are here to ensure you get the support you need, as soon as possible, to reduce the risk of delay." Will spoke for the first time since leaving Long Ridge. "Better communication must add to the strength you speak of, don't you think?"

Alexander narrowed his eyes, but nodded slowly. "That is true. The more men at my disposal, and quickly, the better things will be for everyone. Well, you are here anyway. Make the cottage as comfortable as you are able, and you will be welcome to join us at the bastle for your meals." He turned to Meg. "As agreed."

"We'll be away to make ourselves at home then. Until this evening."

"Oh no, I don't think you'll need to be back this evening. There'll be no grand feast tonight. I'll make sure some food is sent along to you, but I'm sure you wouldn't want to disturb my bride and me on our wedding night, would you?"

The threat was clear, and Meg glanced instinctively at Will.

"No Sir, not at all. Until tomorrow then," Will replied, with a forced politeness.

Meg couldn't help feeling pride building inside her at the clarity of his voice. She wasn't sure she would be so gracious, if their places were reversed. But when Alexander took her hand and went to lead her up the steps into the main body of the bastle, she felt a chill rush through her. The wedding had been one thing. The wedding night, she feared, was going to be quite another.

Her hopes that she might be spared the trauma for that night were dashed when Alexander sent everyone away from the bastle, even banishing Henry to a neighbouring cottage.

"We don't want to be disturbed, do we?" he said, as he made his way to the upper floor of the building.

She forced down a shudder at the smoothness of his voice as she followed him, dreading what she was about to face. No curtaining-off here, Meg noticed, looking around at the wooden panels which divided the room into smaller chambers. Only one had a bed in it; Henry's rooms must be on the floor below. A whole floor's worth of private chambers was certainly impressive; Meg couldn't help but admit that. How she longed for such privacy, and the space to be on her own from time to time, something which simply wasn't possible in Long Ridge's smaller tower house. Everything was just that little bit bigger, better, and more luxurious. Despite herself, she found her eyes focusing on the rich covers of the bed which dominated one of the chambers.

"Don't worry, my sweet, I've done this before. I'll be gentle."

For a moment, she heard a softness in his voice. A glance in his direction showed he was indeed smiling at her, and for once without that predatory glint in his eyes.

"I'm just, well, a little nervous." At least the truth came easily to her.

Alexander put an arm gently around her shoulders. "We both have a duty to do, and I'm glad you know yours, but my main concern is the bastle, and keeping this place secure. You do your share of that, and in this particular department, I'm sure we will find everything perfectly satisfactory. I'll leave you to get ready." He squeezed her shoulders, and for a moment, Meg thought he was going to kiss the top of her head, but then he moved away, disappearing back into the heart of the building.

Alone, Meg looked more closely around the room, taking in the pile of her trunks and bags which had been placed in a corner. Knowing there was no point putting things off, she opened the main trunk, pulling out a number of gowns before finding the nightgown she had brought specifically for that evening. It was beautiful, with an intricately-sewn floral design she had picked herself, and stitched with Hannah's help. It was an important part of the evening, but more so was the tiny package she had secretly stitched loosely into one of the sleeves. She wasn't ignorant of the world; she had seen the stain on the sheet on Will's bed after they had shared it for the first time, and she knew that Alexander would be expecting the same. Pig's blood, in a tiny stitched bladder, would have to suffice, if she could act her part well enough. Ridiculously, she had even rehearsed with Will. She picked away some of the stitches, making it easier to pull away when it was needed. It wouldn't be long now.

Alexander returned to the room just over an hour later, as Meg was finishing sorting what she had assumed was her personal chamber. Fresh linens had been placed on a chair in front of a small desk, with just enough space cleared for her belongings to be set out in an orderly manner.

"Ah, yes, I should have said. The bedchamber isn't really big enough for two peoples' things, and, well, my first wife liked to keep her personal effects in here. Well done," he added, looking at the neatness of the room.

"I know how important it is to have clear space, in case of incidents," she replied, suddenly feeling the need to demonstrate she was more use to anyone than simply a pretty face and the capacity to bear a child.

Alexander nodded, then gestured towards the main bedchamber. Meg walked past him, hoping that she could get away with what she had planned.

Her practising paid off. As her new husband pushed inside her, Meg cried out, clutching him to her with one arm, as, with the other, she slipped her hand into her sleeve for the bladder pouch, crushing it deftly between her legs as he withdrew and rolled away from her. In a moment, he was facing her again.

"Are you well?"

She mumbled a yes, and nodded, keen to look as though she was still slightly in shock at the whole situation.

"Good. Then I suggest we both get some rest ahead of tomorrow – you'll be wanting to get to know your new home." Without another word, Alexander turned his back to her, and pulled the blankets up to his shoulders.

Meg stared blankly at the ceiling, wondering if Will was thinking of her at the same moment. She refused to cry, but the darkness in her heart was threatening to consume her, and she wasn't sure whether the best thing was to allow herself to drift into sleep, or fight to stay awake, keeping the risk of dreams at bay. In the end she had no choice, as sleep eluded her, her mind full of the day, and dreading the morning.

CHAPTER FORTY-ONE

The next morning, Meg studiously avoided making eye contact with Will or Ben as they joined Alexander, herself and Henry to break their fast along with other key members of the Cliffside community. As with Long Ridge, there was a strong sense of the bastle being at the heart of the village, and it did make Meg slightly happier to know there was a sense of community to the place. Alexander was boasting to anyone who would listen about his 'sleepless night' and how content he was with his new young bride, as Meg cringed to herself. At least the women present were being more sympathetic, and everyone could understand why she didn't want to meet the eyes of the two men responsible for keeping in contact with her two brothers on Cliffside's behalf.

"Today, the three of you should get to know the place," Alexander announced. "You two," he said, pointing at Will and Ben, "will go with Hal, whilst you, my love, will go with Sarah."

Meg looked at the woman who, the previous evening had briefly been introduced as Sarah Martin, evidently a well-established member of the Cliffside community, although she had not been part of the group who attended her wedding. The latter now smiled half-heartedly across the table at her, before glancing at Alexander. Following his nod, Sarah's smile grew slightly, but Meg could see no warmth in it.

The two parties set off in opposite directions around the small collection of cottages. Meg trailed after Sarah, wondering what Will was thinking of his new home. The Cliffside people seemed friendly enough, with the possible exception of Sarah, but Meg didn't want to enquire why that might be. The glances between Sarah and Alexander whilst they had been eating suggested something deeper there, and if her husband had a mistress, it wasn't something Meg wanted to know the details of. Instead, she followed dutifully behind as her guide pointed out the homes of people Meg ought to get to know: those who attended market on behalf of the bastle, those who made the best beer or bread, and Elspeth the village's herbalist 'for when you need assistance in family matters.' Everything was so similar to Long Ridge. She was sure she would find her way around soon enough, and know who to go to for what, but Sarah's snippy comments were starting to wear her down, and she had been here for only been a matter of hours.

Finally, they were back within the shelter of the bastle. Regardless of how the other woman might see herself in Alexander's eyes, the bastle was now Meg's domain, and one she was used to, even if Alexander was very different from how Robert and Judd had ever been. However petty it felt, Meg found herself answering back to almost everything Sarah pointed out, whether it be the best way to access the first floor of the building (the outside steps, apart from when the weather was wet or frosty – or when you were escaping your husband, Meg found herself wondering), or the easiest way to protect that same floor (kicking away or burning said outside steps). After all, had she not grown up and led a home almost identical to this for the last twenty and more years? Cliffside might be bigger and have a greater household and village to protect, but the rules – and how she would handle the situations – were the same.

***

Will and Ben were being shown things from quite a different perspective. The best defensive positions, the quickest and safest ways to leave the village in a hurry, and the cottages belonging to the best fighting men, so they could be summoned quickly when required. Will was taking in as much as he could, forcing thoughts of Meg to the back of his mind. Whatever happened now, this was his home, for good or bad, and he had to be able to defend it just as much as he had fought for Long Ridge. More so, in truth, now that there wasn't just Meg to consider, but also their child, even if he'd never be acknowledged as the true father. He would be a guide, a mentor of sorts, he hoped, for the child, especially if it was a boy. The idea of being there for his son brightened him for a moment, as Hal showed them the forge in closer detail. Despite having spent the night there, neither he nor Ben had actually looked around the cottage, simply collapsing into the two beds in the second chamber.

Now, Will saw their new home wasn't quite as derelict as Alexander's sneer the previous evening had suggested. It wasn't luxurious, but it had more space than his small room at Cecily's cottage at Long Ridge, and was comfortable enough, with plenty of blankets to keep them warm at night, and a decent fireplace where they could cook for themselves if they couldn't face going up to the bastle for their meals. Hal pointed out where they could get provisions, and the best place to store their weapons, so they would be in easy reach but not easily accessible should any raider find their way into the cottage.

All in all, it wasn't the life either Ben or Will had planned for themselves, but it could certainly have been far worse. If only he could stop thinking about Meg for more than a few moments at a time.

CHAPTER FORTY-TWO

The rain-drenched wind rattled the thin glass of the bastle's upper windows, as Meg watched clouds scud past each other over the distant hills. She knew she was looking in the right direction for Long Ridge, but the way she was feeling, her former home might as well have been a thousand miles away.

Yes, it had been only three days since her wretched wedding, and yes, the man she loved was, as she looked down on the bigger and better-defended enclosure, less than a hundred feet from her. But trying to be optimistic wasn't helping. Not after having reached the decision she had known she would need to come to, whatever she had hoped.

It was several hours later when she managed to find an opportunity to speak to Will, pulling him into a small alcove in the great hall.

"Is all well?" he asked, glancing down at her stomach for the briefest of moments.

Meg nodded, steadying herself against the wall, suddenly nervous. "I needed to tell you, to ask you, well, no, to tell you, if you haven't realised it yourself yet, that we need to be so careful now. We cannot afford even the slightest mistake, or I fear what will happen to all three of us." She paused for a moment, searching his eyes for a hint of emotion, but they remained calm. "At least for a month, until I tell him about the baby, we need to keep our distance, however much it hurts. You do understand?"

Now she saw the sadness in his dark eyes.

"I want to argue with you, tell you how wrong you are, and what a mad decision it is, but you're right, I do see that," he said, taking half a step back from her as one of Alexander's men entered the other end of the room. "But promise me, go to Ben, if you need anything."

"Does he know?"

"Of the child? No, of course not. Nobody does, but he has eyes, and I think he suspects something, even if he cannot know the half of it."

Not caring who saw for one reckless moment, she reached for his hand. "You must be so careful, Will, please? Nobody must suspect anything."

He squeezed her fingers gently. "My love, it will be fine. He thinks it nothing more than a daft lad going soft for his master's sister. Maybe that is all it is…"

His jest brought her back to her senses. "Oh, you're cruel. But very well. And of course, it is a softening that his master's sister cannot return at all. What a ridiculous notion that would be."

"Ridiculous indeed, my lady." Will glanced around them, checking they were out of full view. In the swiftest of movements, he raised her hands to his lips. "The goodbye won't be forever, but we shall indeed be careful. But don't forget I love you." Without giving her the chance to reply, or cry, he turned away. "Very good, Miss Meg, I'll see to it."

Quite what he was pretending to see to, Meg didn't care, as she fought down the tears that were threatening to flow. With the bastle always having somebody about, she pulled her shoulders back, keen that nobody should see a hint of upset in her demeanour. That wouldn't help anyone's cause. Looking straight ahead, she made her way through the hall, and up into the private rooms.

CHAPTER FORTY-THREE

The next morning, Meg focused, watching a single raindrop plot its course down the panes of glass, joining with others as it went.

"Like a trod," she said, half to herself. It wouldn't be long now, she thought, before the summer reached its peak, and the risk of Cliffside and Long Ridge men being caught up in a trod was at its highest. At least on their own raids, under their own command, there was an element of control. But with a trod, anyone could appear in the village, demand their support, and lead them into who-knew-what danger. She shuddered at the memory of the rout her brothers had ended up in the previous year, and at the thought of poor Andrew and Edward, who had ridden out, not to return. It could have been Will, Meg thought, unhelpfully given her current condition.

A crack of thunder jolted her, and her hand instinctively moved to protect her child. Much as the thought pained her, she wished she could tell Alexander her news sooner. After all, he had already fathered at least one child; he might end up recognising the signs before she told him, over the coming weeks, if he was paying any attention to her diet. Although, Meg considered, at least that would help convince him the baby was his, if he saw the truth before she told him. The two men, Will and Alexander, were similar enough in looks, with the dark hair and brown eyes. He might never suspect a thing, if she kept control of her feelings, and Will could manage his temper when Alexander inevitably lost his. Young Henry was still nursing a black eye from Alexander's fury on their return to Cliffside; she suspected her own child would ultimately have to suffer the same fate.

"Begging your pardon, Miss, but Sir asked me to fetch you." A voice caused Meg to turn round. It was Katherine, a girl whose resemblance to Henry and Alexander was far too close to be a mere coincidence, and whose surname she had never been told.

"Did he say why?" Meg asked, anticipating Katherine's shake of the head; clearly, Alexander Gray was not one to waste his time on giving justification for his orders. With a half-smile, she followed the young girl down the stairs.

He was waiting for her in the hall. "Meg, my darling. A letter from your brothers."

She stepped towards him, moving to take the letter he was holding in his hand, but he tilted it away from her, and continued to read. "Everyone is well, apparently, nothing of significance to report. A minor raid, some new cattle acquired… They've done well by the sound of it. Anyway, I thought you would like to know."

"May I read the letter myself?"

Alexander looked at her as though she had two heads. "I've just told you what Robert writes. There's nothing more to see."

"Still, I should like to see it." She knew Robert's hand well enough, and would be able to see for herself whether it was straight and true, or shaking. If the latter, she would need to determine the cause. Meg kept her focus on Alexander.

He shook his head, then tossed the letter down onto the table. "Very well. But if you are going to be this needy with every communication, you will soon find yourself disappointed. Do you wish to see every word your precious siblings write to you? Will you be planning our raids next?"

She nearly took his bait. She was so close to making it clear to him just how involved she was in the planning at Long Ridge, but knew it was hopeless; Alexander Gray was not the same as her brothers, and certainly wasn't going to accept guidance from a woman of her age. Instead, she fixed her most placid smile across her face, and reached for the letter.

"Thank you, it's very kind of you."

How much longer she could maintain such a level of sweetness was a genuine concern for her.

CHAPTER FORTY-FOUR

As the weeks passed, Meg's aversion to apples remained, and she was aware her dietary preferences were becoming stranger, having found herself looking longingly at the ashen wood remaining in their fireplace one morning. It was now five weeks into her marriage. Watching Alexander go about his day one Sunday, she knew the time had come.

Finally, after church, and dinner in the hall, she got him alone. Her stomach churned, and it wasn't entirely the fault of the bairn.

"Alexander, I have news."

He turned, didn't speak, but gestured for her to continue.

"It is good news. My courses… I mean, I haven't started bleeding as I should have done. I spoke to Elspeth."

"That witch? You let her near you?"

"She said the babe would be born in April. That I looked strong, that all would be well."

At that, he softened slightly, a smile at least spreading across his face. "I shall have another son," said, reaching for her hand.

"If God pleases," Meg replied, carefully not thinking of the child's true father, but glad that he had finally smiled.

"We should tell everyone the good news. And you should write to your brothers and show them how happy you are here, with things progressing as they should. Yes, write to them today. Then we can have more of a reason to push ahead with further plans to the west, now Gloucester has calmed down a little."

"He has?"

"Aye, he's flexed his muscles, and is being kept nicely occupied further to towards the coast. He won't trouble us." Alexander grinned. "You have the most perfect timing, my sweet wife. Well done." He kissed her gently on the forehead, a rare sign of affection, then was back into his usual pace, calling for his men.

Meg picked up the paper, pen and ink from the table, and made her way to the smaller table set against one of the windows, and started thinking of how to share the news with her Long Ridge family.

Meg had hoped that the announcement of her pregnancy would lead to a softening of atmosphere within the bastle at Cliffside. But although Alexander was indeed calmer around her, to an extent, it seemed to have just made him more determined to push ahead with more raids, seemingly intent on gathering more provisions for the child's arrival. Still, it kept him busy, and far too interested in other things to trouble Meg. She wondered whether Sarah was keeping him occupied on the nights he didn't join her in their great bed. The woman was certainly keen to demonstrate whenever she could that her knowledge of Cliffside was far superior than Meg's would ever be. Perhaps that was why poor Bridget had always seemed so cowed, Meg thought, as she watched Sarah at the opposite end of the hall, giving brusque instructions to Katherine. A hint of jealousy, perhaps – if Katherine truly was the result of an illicit affair of Alexander's, it wasn't with Sarah. Meg didn't have the energy to work out who else might have caught Alexander's clearly rather roving eye.

It was Henry's reaction which was causing Meg the most concern. It was true that a second child would have an impact on his inheritance, but Cliffside had sufficient assets to keep two sons comfortably wealthy, if the babe she carried was indeed a son. If it was a girl, then she would end up leaving on her marriage anyway, and financially wouldn't cause her older half-brother any harm at all. She might even marry and bring more wealth to the family. And yet he persisted in making sly remarks when he was certain his father was out of earshot, or placing himself in the most awkward position when she was nearby, making Meg walk around him, or squeeze through the smallest of gaps.

It was Ben, not Meg, who finally rose to the bait.

"Will you not step aside for a lady carrying a child?" he demanded, one evening, as Henry stubbornly failed to acknowledge Meg as she struggled to get round behind his chair.

"I would, but I see no lady: just a woman who sees a good opportunity when it presents itself," the younger man snarled, before hurrying from the room before his father was able to respond.

"He will come around to the idea," said Alexander smoothly. "We should host a meal to celebrate our good fortune, Meg – and show that snivelling boy that sulking will do him no good. You are the lady of this house now, and carrying my child. Both of which, frankly, make you more important than him."

The idea didn't seem one to smooth over the creases in their familial relationships, Meg thought.

"I'm not sure that a celebration will be the best thing for Henry."

"But it will be the best thing for the rest of us. It will be a comparatively quiet affair anyway; after all, we are still in mourning. We will bring some merriment into the bastle for a night. Sarah – see to it that we have the finest of everything possible."

Sarah sat up at the mention of her name, and smirked at Meg, but Meg refused to respond. The more Sarah distracted Alexander, the more chance, in the future, for Meg and Will.

CHAPTER FORTY-FIVE

Days later, Will was the first to see it: the tiniest spot of light, dancing down the hillside in the twilight. It would be hypnotic, beautiful, if he didn't recognise at once what it symbolised. A raid was heading their way.

Even as he rushed into the enclosure, he heard the cry spread through the village, from cottage to cottage, as each family saw the flames, and hurried to tell their neighbours. By the time the troop had reached the edge of Cliffside village, the defence party was assembled.

***

The lights flashed by as Meg watched from the window, hoping the show of strength from the Cliffside men would be enough to warn off the approaching gang. 'Gang' itself was going too far at this stage; it was simply a seething mass of shadow, moving in the rain-drenched twilight, the moonlight occasionally striking the metal of a chest-plate or weapon. They must be desperate, she thought, to be trying an attack in these conditions. Desperate or inexperienced. Neither was a good thing. It wasn't light enough to tell yet if they were Scots or English, but either way, arriving like this, with no word sent in advance, they certainly weren't friends. Any last remnant of hope for that vanished as the flaming torch fell onto the roof of the first cottage.

"Fire!" The shout rose from the throats of the Cliffside community. For a moment Meg wasn't sure if it was a warning to keep the current flames from spreading, or an instruction to let loose the arrows and bullets their own men had been primed with since noticing the group come over the hillside. It was, it turned out, a combination of both.

The shouts and screams raced towards those in the safety of the bastle, as the risk of chaos loomed. However bad it got, they had to stay as calm as they could to keep their chances of surviving this.

Out in the enclosure, she could see Alexander was in his element.

"You two, the rooftop, keep a watch on progress. Shoot any of them within striking distance. You, get the water chain going. Everyone else, full alert!" The instructions came thick and fast, as half the men rushed to quell the flames, half to cut off the raiders before they could advance further into the village. Meg desperately scanned the group, trying to see exactly what was happening.

The jolt of an arrow striking the window frame, inches from Meg's head, brought her rapidly to her senses. This was no time to be an observer. Rushing downstairs and out from the bastle, she joined the group of women, praying they would be safe within the enclosure's walls, frantically raising buckets of water from the well, forming a chain to the fire, now spread to a second building and threatening to go even further.

A piercing scream took them all by surprise. Sensing the metallic tang of blood in the air nearby, Meg turned to seek the source, fearing immediately that Will was wounded. She felt herself pale at the sight which confronted her: Henry. His shirt was already drenched bright red as he was carried roughly into the bastle by two of his comrades. Alexander shot them no more than a passing glance, as Meg and another woman rushed to replace the men, needed elsewhere, and helped his son inside. Meg could feeling him weakening with every step. The wound in his shoulder was cut deep, but it seemed to be a flesh wound only. It was still bleeding heavily, but he would live, if they could staunch the flow then get it cleaned quickly.

The wounding of their leader's son seemed to spur on

the Cliffside men, even if his own father appeared indifferent. They surged forward, now more determined than ever not to be the victims that night. Meg heard the roar of the men as every last one in good health raised their weapons and raced towards their invaders. She wondered if Will was with them, and her hand unintentionally moved to her stomach. Her focus though, was on Henry. Claire Wilson, one of the more reliable women from the village, was currently hurrying from the floor above. Her arms were full of linen strips, her eyes already on the bucket Meg had claimed from the line heading out towards the fire. The water was cold, but it would have to do.

Henry was lying still, almost too still, on a blanket pulled hurriedly from around the shoulders of one of the women. Meg's own cloak had been thrown over him to try and keep him as warm and comfortable as possible.

"Get as much pressure onto that wound as you can," Meg instructed Claire, who was now kneeling next to her at Henry's side. "Come on, Henry, speak to me, I need to you open your eyes and tell me you can still hear me." She spoke with a confidence she didn't feel, as the poor boy murmured, but didn't move. "Henry!" She shouted this time. It was enough.

"Mother?" Henry whispered.

"Not yet, my sweet, not yet," said Claire, gently stroking his face with her free hand. "She doesn't want you joining her just now. You've plenty more to do with us first." The older lady raised her eyes to meet Meg's, and smiled softly. "He'll be alright, pet, you'll see."

Meg increased the pressure on the wound, and allowed herself the briefest of smiles. To think this young man had so nearly become her husband, and was now, in the strangest of ways, her son. And a son she would not give up on, however little his father seemed to think of him.

The flow of blood was slowing now, and to her relief, no other injured men had been brought in for her and

Claire to deal with. Of course, there was another possible reason why that was, but she wouldn't let herself think about that just now. She had to focus on Henry. Claire had applied a slight touch of brandy to his lips, and there was a hint of colour returning, but he was still frighteningly pale.

Outside, the noise began to diminish. The two women looked up as one when Alexander stormed in, assessing the situation in a quick glance. "Will he live?"

"Yes, Sir, he will," replied Claire, smiling up at him. Her smile was not returned.

"There are more injured out there, but he was the worst. See to them as soon as you can with the other women. Half the men have chased off the raiders; they didn't get anything from us, thank heavens. Seems Henry getting shot was almost a distraction." Alexander still wasn't looking at his son with half the concern that Meg felt.

"And you?" She dared ask him.

"Me?"

"Are you injured?"

"Don't be ridiculous. I don't get injured. Nobody would dare." Without another word, he made his way to the floor above, his boots heavy on the wooden boards over their heads.

"He does care, you know," said Claire.

"I'm sure," said Meg, unconvinced.

CHAPTER FORTY-SIX

Meg spent the next three days and nights at Henry's bedside, keeping a close watch on him as he drifted in and out of the much-needed sleep which she hoped would allow him to recover with no major lasting damage. Despite herself, her mind didn't wander once. Henry's arm would be weakened, that was certain, but at least it was not his sword arm. Riding a horse would be a challenge for a while, but she hoped that his father would reduce the need for that, letting Henry stay closer to home.

Gradually, the boy became stronger.

"Meg?"

She smiled. At least he had stopped calling her 'Mother'; that had been a little too unnerving, not to mention the sign that his mind was still wandering. Her smile didn't last long, as his face formed itself into a scowl as Henry focused on her.

"I want you to leave me alone."

"What?"

"Let Claire care for me. I don't trust you."

Meg recoiled, her hand paused on its way to wrap fresh cloth around his wound. "Henry?"

"I mean it. Send Claire. Now." His voice was weak, but the words were strong enough.

Shocked, Meg rose from her place, and left the room to find Claire where she had last seen her, out in the enclosure.

Finding one of her few friends at Cliffside, Meg explained what had happened. Claire frowned, but held her close when she finished, as though sensing the tears were about to flow.

"But why?" Meg asked, between sobs.

"Come, lass, it's nothing. It's not long since he lost his mother, and now you're here. You know what sort of woman Bridget was. A good one, kind, and loving to that poor boy, whatever his father was putting him through."

Meg nodded into Claire's shoulder, then pulled away, wiping her eyes with the flats of her hands. "It was always going to be difficult, coming here, being his 'mother' of sorts, wasn't it?" Quite apart from the fact that his father was a tyrant, and Meg's mind was almost constantly on somebody else. Without thinking, her hand returned to her stomach.

Claire smiled. "That's right, my pet, you concentrate on bringing that new life of yours into the world. A young brother or sister might just be the thing which brings Henry back to us all, and back to your side. Might bring some cheer to the whole place." Patting Meg's hand, Claire bustled by, to the boy Meg knew she had watched grow up.

This lady was Cliffside's version of Hannah; Meg had seen that in the way the villages deferred to her in discussions and opinions. Even Alexander had been known to take her advice, and that, according to what Meg had learned so far, was practically unheard of. Even Bridget had never managed to make her opinion heard to her tyrannical husband.

Walking back into the bastle, Meg made her way to the partitioned area of the uppermost floor which formed the bedroom she shared with Alexander. She perched on the windowsill, glancing down at the village below, trying to pick out which light might be Will's, before he bedded down for the night in the tiny cottage he and Ben had been assigned. There were so many similarities between Cliffside and Long Ridge, and yet, she doubted it would ever have the same feeling as her beloved home. Yes, there had been plenty of raids over the years, and Long Ridge would always be the place where she had lost her parents, the ones who had treasured her most in the world, but there were the happy memories too. Memories of them all growing up together, until Judd went off to seek fortune and adventure, of Judd rejoining them after the loss of their parents, of the successful raids and the triumphant feasting.

Then there was Will. How had somebody she hardly knew come to have such an effect on her? One injured ankle and she had found her destiny. She laughed at the ridiculousness of it all; he had been nothing but another one of Robert and Judd's men – and yet here she was, having just announced his baby as her husband's. A husband which most certainly was not Will, and whose character bore no resemblance to him whatsoever, despite their physical similarities.

She looked out in the direction of Long Ridge. The news had arrived there of her pregnancy; she knew that from Ben and his regular visits. There had been a brief letter from her brothers, congratulating her and Alexander, and sending her their fondest love. There had been nothing from Hannah, but Meg knew she wasn't the greatest with her letters, struggling to write anything beyond a list of goods to take to market. It would have been encouraging to hear from the woman who had been part-mother, part-sister, but that was the way life was.

Men's voices disturbed Meg's thoughts. She turned away from the window as Alexander entered with Hal.

"Husband? Can I help you?"

"What? No. Just replacing something." Alexander moved to the end of the bed as Hal held up the mattress.

"What are you doing?" Meg asked, her eyes widening as she saw a locked panel in the bedstead. "How long has that been there?"

"Longer than you have, my dear; longer than I have, in all honesty. Did you never wonder where our ammunition was kept?"

"Ammun… You cannot mean I have been sleeping for this last two months over… over bullets? They could have exploded. They could have killed us."

"This bastle has kept an emergency store of ammunition under this bed for as long as I've been alive," replied Alexander. "Whenever we use it up, we ensure it's replenished." He nodded to Hal, who opened the box he had been carrying, to reveal its secret. "Brand new. This will mean we're never caught without the means to defend ourselves. And they've never exploded yet."

She watched as the two men placed the ammunition into the cavity, and replaced the locked panel before covering it with the mattress. "You are beyond lucky that your own bed has never killed you," she muttered.

Alexander shrugged. "Better watch your evening candle then, hadn't you?" He leaned in to kiss her before she could move away, his arm pulling her closer.

She forced herself to soften, and return the smile he gave her as he moved away. "Just remember there are three of us sleeping here now, won't you?"

That worked. His eyes glinted at the reference to the child. She could see a tenderness which must have existed in him, once, and wondered whether Bridget had kindled it when she told him they were expecting Henry. Meg desperately wanted to find something to like in this man, even if she knew she would never love him. Perhaps the tenderness for a new-born would be it.

CHAPTER FORTY-SEVEN

Meg's hopes for a permanent softening of Alexander's attitude rose further the next morning, with his surprise announcement.

"A feast?" She looked him directly in the eye, but couldn't see a trace of sarcasm or malice.

"Yes. A feast. We have been in mourning for so long. Even our wedding was held quietly. Well, now we have two things to celebrate. Three, if you count Henry's return to health, and a generally successful start to the season – we are prosperous thus far. So why not a feast, show the world we are strong, happy, and secure? Cliffside's show of face to the world."

Meg couldn't help but smile, despite the misgivings racing through her mind. But if Alexander was planning to celebrate her pregnancy, then he must absolutely have believed, without any trace of doubt, that the child was his. She had managed to convince him of her virtue, and now, of her immediate fertility.

"Well then, it sounds a wonderful idea. Perhaps if Claire and I went to Hexham and gathered some special supplies at market, we could make it a night to remember?"

Alexander nodded. "Of course, go to market. But take either Ben or Will with you. I want everyone to see we are still a show of strength at Cliffside."

At his suggestion, Meg felt her heart leap. "An excellent idea. I'll see to it at once. Claire and I will go to market the day after tomorrow." Her mind began racing ahead with plans, the glorious opportunity of a day where she could actually relax, enjoy Will's company, even the luxury of catching up with friends she hadn't seen since moving to Cliffside, when she realised Alexander hadn't stopped speaking.

"… at least with plenty of men with you, there'll be no risk to Cliffside. I won't let people think our strength is reducing."

"I'm sorry, plenty of men?"

"Were you even listening?" His previous pleasant mood had vanished.

"I…"

"Oh, don't trouble yourself to pay attention, what would be the use? You will be escorted by a full troop of men, at least twenty, a full show of strength. Nobody would dare disturb your day to the market, and it will also show everyone that a new Gray is about to enter the world. The perfect indication that all is well. And whilst you are there, be sure to show you're buying enough food and drink for a feast. We shall have ourselves a fine banquet, to celebrate the announcement of a new arrival."

Meg's heart sank at the notion of spending an entire day under the watchful eye of Alexander's mob of thugs.

Her fears were proved correct, as she and Claire were hurried around the various market stalls. This was nothing like the slow, fun meanderings that Meg and Hannah had always enjoyed, once the work of the day was done. And it wasn't just being there with a relative stranger with Claire, Meg thought, as she missed her friend's company; there was also a distinct change in atmosphere. She and Hannah had often received friendly nods and greetings from the people they saw every couple of weeks, or knew well as friends and neighbours, but the attitude now was different. The smiles were more cautious, the greetings more subdued. Whenever she caught somebody's eye, their glance would pass across the accompanying retinue, before shyly nodding and scurrying away.

"Is this always the way it is on market day?" Meg asked Claire, leaning towards her companion, in a low voice.

Claire glanced around at the men, and shook her head. "It's since, you know, Bridget. The rumours haven't quite died as Alexander would have liked."

Meg sighed. "Nor will they, if those who say anything too loudly keep ending up in trackside ditches."

"Do not say that!" hissed Claire. "Please. It would be risky even for us. Even for you."

Meg took her warning, hurrying them through the rest of their purchases and returning to Cliffside as quickly as possible. Before now, this was not something she had ever considered doing.

CHAPTER FORTY-EIGHT

If Alexander was worried about the rumours which were rushing around Northumberland about him, he wasn't showing it that evening. The Cliffside bastle was alight, with the finest candles brought out for the occasion, glinting off the highly-polished silverware and pewter. A few of Alexander's neighbours had been invited to share the celebrations, although not (Meg noted with some sadness) Robert or Judd. Clearly Alexander didn't feel the need to try and impress either of her brothers. The wine and ale were flowing, the music almost drowning out the majority of the conversations, and food covered every table.

Meg forced herself to at least look as though she was enjoying herself, but if she was being honest with herself, she was full of nerves. She watched as Will and Ben sat side-by-side with Alexander's men, sharing food and drink, and had a sense that they were feeling partly the same. She saw that none of their smiles reached their eyes.

In the commotion of the celebrations, somehow, nobody had noticed Henry remaining in his chamber for the bulk of the evening, only emerging to collect a plate of food from the table. The lad was still sullen from the latest argument with his father – although it was anyone's guess what had happened this time, Meg thought, as the fights had been becoming far more frequent. Meg watched him prowl around the room, occasionally glancing her way, his face filled with hatred. From the slight sway to his step, it was clear he had been drinking.

"Alexander, I worry for Henry. Is he quite well?" she whispered into her husband's ear, hoping that he would give the lad some attention at the thought of him being ill. She was out of luck.

"Henry! Boy, what's the matter with you, are you

drunk? If so, then I hope it is out of celebration, at the imminent arrival of a new sibling for you."

Henry spun to face them both.

"You would truly replace every scrap of her, of both of us?" he shouted at the top of his voice, bringing the celebrations to an instant halt, as all eyes turned to the three of them, facing each other across the great hall. "You kill my mother, replace her by stealing my own bride, then plan to replace me too, with the child of your whore!"

The silence was broken only by a few brave gasps of horror as the insult was taken in by his audience. Alexander moved slowly to narrow the space between him and his son. Meg was frantic, but felt unable even to breathe.

"Care to repeat yourself, son?" Alexander said, slowly, his words dripping with menace.

"You heard me, father." Henry pulled himself up to his full height, all shadow of his former nerves gone, clearly brimming with some new confidence, however ill-placed. "You have insulted me in every way imaginable. You killed my mother. Everyone here knows it; they're just too terrified of you to say anything. As was I, until the day you did it, and took this… this girl to replace her. She was meant to be mine, but you couldn't stand the thought of me having somebody worth having, so you got rid of a good woman and stole this one for yourself. And now, she's pregnant. How wonderful, how convenient, that you won't be needing me anymore. So what, I'm the next to be replaced?"

"You should watch your tongue, boy, have a care," warned Alexander, now less than a yard from Henry, his hand hovering dangerously close to the hilt of his sword.

Henry evidently hadn't noticed, seemingly blind with fury. He continued his rant at his father, letting every last bit of hatred he had bottled up inside for so long flow out in a great torrent. Meg watched as Alexander's eyes grew colder and colder, until with one accusation too many, he raised his hand and went to slap his son hard across the face. Henry must have realised at that exact moment what was going to happen, and instantly drew the knife he kept in his belt and lashed out at his father's hand as it flew towards his face.

The moment seemed to stand still. The knife connected with the back of Alexander's hand, cutting a straight wound. In that instant, Henry's face paled, as though he hadn't realised what he had done. He turned in an attempt to make his escape from the bastle, but he wasn't quick enough. His father drew his sword from at his hip, and launched for the boy. Henry grabbed out for anything to defend himself, and pulled his father's beloved Sarah out in front of his body. Meg watched, horrified, as Alexander swiftly spun Sarah out of the way and into her father's arms, his eyes not once leaving Henry's movement across the room.

Henry was at the end of the table now, standing beside Meg, his knife at her throat.

She froze. Even as the daughter and sister of a reiver, she had never suffered a threat to her physical safety, only ever to her possessions. Now, feeling the chill of the blade, all she could do was stay still, and hope that the boy had enough of his wits about him not to accidentally slit her throat as he stepped away from her, as his father was commanding him to do.

"I will not move, father. Why shouldn't I just slit her throat, here and now? At least it would be honest, rather than pushing her down the stairs whilst nobody was looking, so she was just found one morning, without any love or dignity!" Henry pushed the blade of his knife closer against the skin of Meg's neck, so close to cutting her that Meg held her breath, for fear the movement would make the knife break the skin. She could feel her pulse pounding, as she willed her body to stay still.

"You will step away, boy, slowly, or face the consequences of your actions."

Henry pushed the blade closer. "I will n—"

Henry's words were cut off by a deafening bang. For a moment, Meg thought the house was going to fall down around them, as though it had been struck by lightning. Then she saw Will. He was standing behind Alexander, slightly to his left, holding a smoking pistol. Slowly, she turned to where Henry had been standing. With a wave of relief, she saw that he was still breathing. Clearly Will had aimed for his arm, and was skilled enough to hit where he intended.

The boy grabbed at his arm, his hand slipping on the blood which was now flowing freely, as Meg's instinct kicked in, running through her veins as it had done on so many occasions before when she had needed to bandage the injuries of her brothers or one of their men. She ripped the sleeve from her dress, and went to tie it above the wound, as she had been taught, to stem the flow of blood, when Alexander suddenly called to her.

"Leave it," he commanded.

"But he could lose the arm," Meg protested, surprising even herself for the care she felt for the young man who could easily have killed her with one swift slash of his knife less than a minute ago.

"Leave it. He has caused this himself. If he wants treating, he can do that himself too." Alexander's eyes looked as though they had turned black with anger, and Meg could do nothing but leave Henry whimpering like a kicked dog at her side. He met her eyes briefly, before dragging himself to his feet, and staggering from the upper level, drips of blood marking his path as the crowd parted, as though they did not want to risk being tainted by the hatred he had caused in his father.

Only when Henry had left the room, did Alexander turn to Will.

Will had let his arm drop to his side, but his hand still clutched the gun, as though he felt he may need to use it once more, even if only as a club, with no time to reload and fire again.

"You shot my son."

"Sir, forgive me, I could not see my mistress in danger," Will's voice was steady, even as he met Alexander's eyes.

"He may lose the arm if the bleeding does not cease, your mistress herself said that."

"The knife, sir. If his hand had slipped…"

"You should have aimed for his heart," said Alexander, spinning on his heel and barging his way through the crowd to the window.

Feeling herself begin to shake with the shock of what had happened, Meg followed him unsteadily. He was looking out of the tall slit window, down to the enclosure, where Henry was trying to mount his horse with only one useful arm, and clearly in a lot of pain.

"If he doesn't get help soon he could bleed to death," she said quietly so that only her husband could hear.

"He deserves it," Alexander replied under his breath. "I only wish I'd done it myself rather than letting your man Will take the glory."

"You can't mean that, he is your son," Meg implored him. She could not stand by and allow him to let his son die.

"I can have more sons," Alexander growled, turning back from the window. "Now," he called to the rest of the room, "I do believe this is a feast, and we are celebrating news of my wife's pregnancy. So, who shall top up my ale?"

The throng of people looked nervously at one another, as though nobody was brave enough to be the first to attempt to restart the merriment. How could they eat, drink and be merry when Henry Gray was most likely bleeding to death somewhere out in the darkness? But their master called for more ale, and eventually Sarah, gestured by Meg, stepped forward with a pitcher and filled his mug.

"Well then, a toast! To Meg, and the safe arrival of my child!" he called, raising his mug.

"To Meg," came the half-hearted reply.

But Alexander didn't appear to hear it; his eyes glazed over as he seemed to stare at nothing at all.

Meg watched in silent horror as he joined her again at the window and looked down as his son limped away. Henry had given up trying to get on his horse, and was simply struggling to the village, where Meg prayed there would somebody who had been too ill or frail to make it to the bastle for the festivities. But as she looked around, she could identify no missing faces among the crowd.

CHAPTER FORTY-NINE

The mood in the bastle had changed irreversibly, but Alexander refused to let the matter lie. For the rest of the evening nobody left the building, for any reason. Meg knew that whatever reason they might have tried to give, everyone just wanted to try and find Henry before it was too late, and give him the chance his father had refused him.

His body was found the next morning, when Alexander finally called a halt to proceedings, having forced merriment on his people for almost twelve hours, with the first hints of sunlight already starting to pierce the horizon. As Ben walked through the village with the family who had taken to helping feed him and Will, hoping for some sleep before the day's work began, their young daughter tripped and fell over an obstacle on the pavement. Ben called at once for torches, and as the flames cast their light on the ground, even he recoiled in horror. Henry hadn't even made it properly to the village. He had fallen, and in his weakened state hadn't had the strength to pull himself up again.

When the news was brought to the bastle, Alexander hardly looked up from breaking his fast. Meg was distraught. She had not liked Henry much, that was for sure, but had hoped deep down that they would eventually form some sort of friendship, even if only a civil accord. Without thinking, she placed her hand over her stomach. It was still so small, but her feelings of thankfulness that her child would have a wealthy and content upbringing (even if it could never know its true father) had fallen apart in the space of a day. How could she think about bringing a child into the world, when the man who believed he was its father thought nothing of the death of his only legitimate son?

Will's arrival in the room did nothing to soothe her, as she took the excuse of sickness to rush away to the privacy of the main bedchamber and escape the oppressive atmosphere in the hall.

That afternoon, when Alexander had taken himself, Hal and some of his men out for a ride, Meg crept out to the forge to find Will and Ben sat at their table, each staring into a mug of ale. Both went to rise as she approached, but Meg waved their gesture away as she joined them, reaching for a third mug and filling it for herself.

"I did not mean to kill him," said Will, as though he had been repeating it all day to anyone who would listen. "I meant only to disarm him. He had a knife at your throat. Your brothers would have killed me if I had allowed him to harm you."

"I know," said Meg, trying to sound calming, wanting nothing more than to put her hand on his, to pull him close and tell him everything would be alright. She could see Will was blaming himself entirely for Henry's death, and there was bound to be a lot of talking done tonight. Although that was probably true for every home in the village. And further afield by now, if she knew the speed gossip could fly in these parts. She could only hope Alexander would stay away for a good few hours yet. "Look, Alexander is as much to blame as you. More so. If he had let me tend the wound, Henry would be alive now, I know it. You did disarm him, and Robert and Judd would not have looked kindly upon you if you hadn't."

"That's what I keep telling him," said Ben. "Exactly what I keep telling him."

"I've dealt with worse injuries than that, and the men have lived. You did not kill him." Meg realised she didn't care what Ben might think. Putting down her mug, she rose to kneel beside Will, taking his face in her hands and making him look at her. "You are not to blame."

"But what of Gray?" Will mumbled, tearing his face away from her grip. "He may not show anger now, but soon enough he'll realise he's lost his son, his adult son, and then he'll come for me."

"I will not let him harm you," Meg promised, yet even as the words left her mouth, she wondered what she could possibly do to prevent it.

"I want you to promise me something, Meg," said Will, the life suddenly returning to his eyes, as he leaned forward in his chair. "If anything happens to me, or to Ben, you get out of here, do you understand? You grab one of our horses, and you run back to Long Ridge like the path's on fire behind you. Robert and Judd would never question you, you know that, and they wouldn't let Gray anywhere near you, not once they knew the truth about how bad things were here, and what he's really like. You promise me?"

Meg nodded, not wanting to admit that she was already thinking the same thing. The only difference was that she was contemplating her escape if something happened to anyone, not just Ben or her beloved Will.

It didn't take long for the sadness following Henry's death to turn to anger. Alexander's started as a quiet, seething fury, as though he had begun to realise that the son he had lost could take a long time to replace, if at all. He constantly referred to Meg's still-small but growing stomach as his new son. No strange reaction for a man, but the malice behind it was starting to make his wife nervous. It was clear Alexander blamed Meg at least in part for the lad's demise, but she knew that in his eyes she was now the only one who could put things right.

Half her days were now spent with her hand across her ever-growing bump, as though she might protect whoever was in there from the world, and from the man who would be his or her acknowledged father.

She did hope, deep down, that it would be a boy. A

fine young man, who could be taught by his 'Uncle' Will, as well as his true uncles, Robert and Judd. Meg didn't want to think about what Alexander would teach the child. That was what made her angry. Angry, and afraid that if a man could kill one son, and most probably his first wife, what would stop him doing it again? Angry, and jealous of Hannah, who got to stay at Long Ridge, happy with the man she loved. Angry, and sad, that her own brother hadn't seen the situation he was sending her to. The negative emotions flooded through her to the point that she worried she would somehow harm her beloved child, but all that did was spin her hurt and anger even more out of control.

She was starting to wonder how much more of it all she could take.

CHAPTER FIFTY

Meg looked on in shock as two of her husband's most favoured men, the Robson brothers, staggered into the bastle's lower level, as she checked the horses for the night.

"Hal! John! What happened? Are we under attack?" With half her attention on the two men, she rushed past them to the door, staring out for any obvious danger, but seeing none.

Hal snorted a bark of laughter, causing blood to spray from his mouth and nose onto the hem of Meg's dress. Both men mumbled apologies as she ushered them up to the main hall, telling them she would have all the details once the bleeding had stopped.

It wasn't what she expected. Muffled by the scraps of linen she ordered them to hold in place over his nose, Hal sputtered his way through the course of events.

"Went mad, he did. Started yelling at us, saying it was our fault."

"What? Henry?"

John nodded, as Hal continued.

"We were all there; everyone saw what happened. You saw what happened. But I think he's past reason. He started lashing out, throwing things, when we were over at the forge."

At the mention of Will and Ben's home, Meg's panic increased. "The forge? Was anyone else injured?"

"No, we were the only fools to get in his way." The older man paused for a moment. "You have a care, with the little one to think about now, won't you?"

For the first time, Meg looked at Hal properly. He wasn't as rowdy as some of the others, with the steady, evenness of age giving him a quiet strength. His blue eyes were pale now, and she suspected it was from more than the pain. She placed her hand over his, and smiled with what she hoped was encouragement.

"I'm sure I will be fine." Inside, though, her heart raced. If Alexander was storming around the village, indiscriminately lashing out at his own men, she feared for Will's safety. Their vow to stay away from each other had come to nothing after all. Once Hal and John were seen to, she made her way out to the forge as soon as she could.

The forge looked deserted as she approached. "Will?" she hissed through the darkness.

"Meg, is that you?"

She relaxed for a moment at the sound of his voice, then the sense of dread hit her. "Were you here, when Alexander went on his rampage?"

Will shook his head. "Ben and I slipped out the back. Some of our belongings took our place." He picked up the remains of his spare dagger, split in half, the forge's axe still lying on the table.

"I cannot risk this any longer. I want you gone by the morning." The words came out so quickly she surprised herself, let alone Will. She raised her hand as Will went to protest. "No. Look, this hurts me far more than you imagine, but it's too dangerous. Look what he's just done to Hal and John, and they are men he's known for years, men he trusts. Will, I can hardly trust myself to even look at you, when all I want every day is to creep down here and spend every moment I can with you. If he suspects anything, for a moment, it will be the end for both of us. For all three of us." She rushed to the end of her sentence, knowing she had to get the words out.

"No. No, I'm not leaving you here, not with that madman. Even being a loyal resident isn't enough to protect anyone," Will argued, clearly struggling to keep his voice calm.

Meg wasn't as controlled. "Will, please! It isn't safe. You saw what happened."

"But you—"

"I am his wife, and carrying his new son. I am currently the only hope he has for a legitimate child. He won't touch me." Meg hoped Will believed her. She hoped she would believe herself. "You have to leave."

"Think how it would look. Surely, if he suspects anything, me running away would only make it worse?"

Meg closed her eyes and turned away from him. "You have to leave," she repeated, her voice barely above a whisper, as tears began to flow down her cheeks. "I'm safe – you are the one in danger. And I'll still have Ben."

Will dropped onto the bed, his head in his hands. "What sort of man am I, who takes order after order from his lover?"

"The sort of man who knows it is more important to keep himself safe for the sake of his unborn child. The sort of man who I love more than anyone or anything else in this world." Meg's face was wet with tears now, but her voice was strengthening. "You are more use to me safe, alive and well in Long Ridge, than in danger here. Please, be gone by morning. Ben and I will think up a reason."

"Cecily."

"What?"

"Tell anyone who asks, that Cecily sent for me. It's as good an excuse as any. I may as well swap orders from one woman for another." He looked up at her, the smallest hint of a smile playing on his lips. "One of these days, you'll do as I tell you," he added, the smile growing.

"One day. Perhaps. But I wouldn't wager anything on it," Meg replied, stooping to kiss him.

Will shook his head. "It's a good thing that I love you."

"Likewise. My world is empty without you, but I would rather it be a little dull for a while, and know you are safe. You'll be back. This little one won't have long without you." She pulled Will's hand onto the slight bump now evident under her gown.

In a moment, he had pulled her towards him, sitting

beside him on the bed. "We need a proper goodbye, don't you think?"

With a final glance at the door to check they were safe, Meg sank back onto the bed.

CHAPTER FIFTY-ONE

By the time Meg woke in Alexander's bed the next morning, she knew Will would be back in Long Ridge. Whether or not anyone would believe that Cecily had summoned her brother back home was a slight concern for her, but she had a feeling that Hannah and Judd suspected enough of her and Will's attraction by now to accept it as a credible reason for the pair to be separated.

"You've lost one of your escorts," said Alexander, coming into the chamber and throwing on his jacket.

"I heard something about his sister wanting him back," Meg replied, deliberately holding his gaze. "But as you rightly said, I didn't really need them in the first place." It was the perfect comment.

"Well, quite. My men are quite strong enough."

"Have you seen Hal or John this morning?" Not such a perfect comment.

He paused, and glowered at her. "How I deal with the behaviour of my men is my business, and not yours, not for a moment. I am aware they came running to you to be patched up, which is a kindness they didn't deserve."

"I'm sorry, but I cannot help wanting to help people; I have a nurturing instinct."

"Then I hope you can focus it more appropriately when we have our child to consider."

Meg saw her chance. "When we have our child, he will have all of my attention, I assure you."

Finally, Alexander half-smiled at her. "For a while, until he has brothers or sisters."

Meg nodded, though the thought of actually carrying Alexander's child, or children, was causing panic to rise in her chest. Luckily, her husband was already moving on.

"There is a rumour the Wardens are on the move this week. We need to be ready if they visit here. Some fool has been spreading lies about me, and I suspect we shall be blessed with their presence."

"Lies? What lies?" Meg pulled herself up in the bed.

"The same old nonsense: that Bridget's death was not an accident."

"I thought there had been an investigation, before we married?"

Alexander shook his head. "The deputy came, asked ridiculous questions, irritated everyone, and wouldn't accept the truth. I had assumed the matter was closed, but clearly not. If I find the man who has been spreading these rumours, believe me, he will be sorry."

Meg didn't doubt that. "What do you need from me?"

Alexander looked at her closely. "You'll help me?"

"You are my husband. You have my duty and loyalty."

"Then I want you at my side, in your best dress. You weren't here when the accident happened, so you cannot add anything there, but be the finest hostess, and make them welcome. I know you're skilled at that, so let's use that to our advantage. I want this over and done with."

"Will you be called to a Day of Truce?"

"No. I won't let it come to that. You do your job, and this will be the end of it."

The Warden's deputy finally arrived two days later, without the man himself. Jarvis rode into Cliffside on his huge horse, with a retinue of twelve armed soldiers to support him. None of them looked as though they were in the mood for an evening of light refreshments and music, as Alexander had made Meg plan.

"If you're trying to fob me off with entertainment, then I'm disappointed in you, Gray," Jarvis said, casually throwing his hat and jacket onto a chair by the fire in the hall.

Alexander was charm personified, Meg observed, as she approached with a jug of ale, Sarah following behind with cups for everyone.

"Fob you off, Sir? But for what purpose? I understand you are here to discuss again the tragic loss of my wife. But you must understand, I am doubly grieving now, following the death of my son just a few short weeks ago. Need we go through this again?"

Jarvis was clearly unmoved, as Meg listened for what felt like the hundredth time to her husband's explanation of how his poor, tired exhausted wife had gone for a walk, inexplicably, in the middle of the night, and tragically lost her footing when, for reasons beyond him, she had decided to use the outside stairs.

Meg realised then that the mighty Alexander Gray had a giveaway when he was lying. She had seen him do it when telling the most inconsequential of untruths, but seeing it now made her blood run cold. He was twisting the ring on his little finger, round and round, as though he didn't even know he was doing it.

That was it, then, she thought. It had definitely been murder.

Instinctively her hands went to her stomach, anything to protect her little one from the monster that was going to be its father.

At last Jarvis and his men left, riding off, no doubt, to try and catch somebody doing something illegal to compensate for not being able to pin Gray down. But Meg didn't rate their chances highly. She watched as Alexander stalked around the upper floor of the bastle, the pair having retreated as soon as they could. Well, as soon as Alexander could, and Meg following his barked order to do so. If things weren't so dire, she would have been amused at Sarah's disgruntled reaction to their disappearance so early in the evening. Meg knew there would be no romance in store between her and Alexander that night, and was grateful for it.

"Will you come to bed?" The words were out of her mouth before she realised exactly what she was asking him. "I mean, I'm sorry, I don't mean, I just – you look worn out, after today. The Warden or his deputy will say and do whatever pleases them, and there's nothing you can do in this moment to change that."

"What? Do you believe that? Do you truly believe I couldn't send half the village after that half-wit and his idiot soldiers, within the hour, and make absolutely sure that they change their mind?"

"I…"

"Of course I could. You forget who you are married to, Margaret Gray, and I would advise that you try harder to remember."

Meg shrank back from him, for the first time not just wary of him, but truly afraid. "I do not forget, I assure you of that."

"Good. You need to forget this silly affection you have for your brothers, and the others at Long Ridge. You're the mistress of Cliffside now, and you need to act like it. You could learn from Sarah."

"Sarah? She's the true mistress here, isn't she?" Meg immediately regretted her words, as Alexander spun around to face her.

"You dare accuse me? I am the master of this household, and I shall do what I wish. I think you ought to go to bed, but I… I have changed my mind. I will see you in the morning."

Without another word, he was gone – no doubt, Meg thought, to Sarah's bed. She wasn't even slightly angry about that.

It was almost a relief the following week, when, after she had spent days treading so carefully around him, Alexander actually shouted at her. It had been over nothing, almost like one of those stupid, childish arguments she had had with Robert when they were small. A throwaway remark over the meal Meg had prepared, that she had apparently taken the wrong way, and for once, for whatever reason, responded in kind: if she had better meat to work with, Alexander would have better meals to dine on. She had even said it with a smile, an attempt to lighten the mood which had seemed to descend every night since Henry's death. Gone were the celebratory, boisterous meals, where drinks and tales flowed well into the night, where laughter filled the hall. Never Meg's laughter, only Alexander's and his men's, but still, laughter was better than what she was having to put up with now.

But the remark about the meat was clearly a step too far. Alexander spun in his seat at her words, fixing her with his coldest stare.

"The meat I provide isn't good enough? Your beloved brothers would do better, would they? I don't see them spurring their horses on to take me on the fells, or coming up with any new ideas to improve our lot. Do you?" His eyes never left her face.

"I just… I mean… I didn't mean…" Meg faltered.

"No, please, am I not good enough for you? You replace my wife, kill my son, and now you insult me as well?"

Meg physically stepped back, shocked at his accusations. "Replace Bridget? I had no… I mean… And kill your son? I tried to save your son!"

"Ha! A pointless gesture that would have been, even if you could have done it. He was a waste of the air he breathed, and certainly not even worth this slop for his meal." Alexander threw the bowl down onto the stone floor, watching it as it shattered, the meat and gravy splattering his legs. "You'll be wanting to clear that up," he snarled. "And there will be laundry needing doing in the morning." He rose, turning to the men who had remained silent throughout. "I suggest we adjourn, take a ride over to Hexham, and find our refreshment in a tavern this evening." Without another word from anyone, the men gathered their cloaks and left the room, leaving Meg still holding the jug of wine she had intended to use to replenish her husband's cup. As though sensing they should follow suit, the women filed out behind them.

Alone, she sank into her chair, using the wine to fill her own cup, and drinking deeply. The warmth of the rich red wine spread through her, welcome against the chill of fear which began to spread through her. Her hand went to her stomach.

"At least if he's away for the night, that's a whole night where it's just you and me, little one," she whispered. "I'll tell you stories again." She didn't know if the child could hear her or not, but telling the tales of its grandfather, her beloved father, soothed Meg as much as if the baby was alert to her words. Anything to break the deafening silence of the Cliffside bastle.

CHAPTER FIFTY-TWO

It was a sign of things to come. Meg could see that clearly, waking the next morning to find Alexander's side of the bed once again empty, but his pile of clothes waiting for her to deal with. Seeing Sarah's smirk of triumph as Meg entered the main hall was enough to make her want to scream, but Alexander had been right about one thing: Meg was the mistress of Cliffside (in name at least), and she had to act like it.

"Good morning. I presume you know where my husband and his men are?" Meg asked, gesturing around the empty room. "And you can also let me know what you are doing here so early in the morning."

"I'm simply doing as the master requested, and preparing his favourite soup for lunch, when he and the men return from checking the boundaries." Sarah continued to bustle around the table, demonstrating her knowledge of the bastle and its main resident.

"You'll have to teach me – I'm always keen to learn how to please my husband, as you can imagine," said Meg, her words practically dripping with sweetness. "You're obviously central to everyone's happiness here."

At Meg's words, Sarah seemed to increase in height by a few inches, and a smile spread across her face. "I've been here longer than anyone. Bridget never appreciated me, nor my importance."

"I wouldn't want to make that mistake, I'm sure."

Sarah paused in preparing the vegetables she had gathered on the table, and looked directly at Meg for the first time. "He isn't a man to be messed with. He likes things his way, and no changing anything without his permission."

"Do you love him?" Meg didn't realise until now just how much she wanted to know the answer.

Sarah shrugged. "No space for love in this world, my dear. He looks after me, and being unmarried, at my age, that's good enough for me. And if I can keep him entertained and happy, the better things are for me."

Meg smiled, and nodded. Another person frightened of her monster of a husband, but at least this one seemed to make the most of the situation. "Do you need any help?" She gestured to the table of ingredients.

Sarah stiffened. "No. This is my triumph, not yours. You and your growing belly can keep him happy in your own way, but don't you dare go trying to steal my victories, when they come."

"I didn't mean—"

"Of course you did. You've got your wedding band, your name, your house; leave me something, or I'll be no better than the women he finds on market day."

The anger in Sarah's face was enough of a warning for Meg, who slipped down through the bastle and into the village. With most of the men gone with Alexander, only the women remained, and none of them were likely to start speaking to her, thanks to the poison she was sure Sarah had been dripping into everyone's ears. Seeking solitude, she made her way to the forge and sat on the workbench outside, her feet on the stool next to it, absent-mindedly playing with the various tools which didn't seem to have moved since Will and Ben had moved in.

Will. Meg almost wished she hadn't thought of him. Even such a short time without him had been agonising. "To think I once hated him," she mused, half to herself, half to her child. "He was so irritating, and self-righteous. You'll know what I mean when you meet him," she continued. "But he's a good man, and I love him, and you will too."

The sound of men's voices broke through her calmer mood; they were returning from riding out. Not wanting to be found in what was now Ben's home, she hurried out the back, and round the perimeter of the village, ready to greet them as they approached the enclosure. Alexander was riding ahead of the rest of his men, as usual, the sun glinting off the silver studs in his black clothing. She had never seen him wearing anything different.

"Good morning, Alexander. I trust all is well at the boundary?"

He looked down at her, and nodded. "A little trouble out to the west, but either myself or Gloucester will be able to deal with that, whoever gets there first."

His arrogance was shocking. That he could even dare count himself in the same breath as a royal duke, the King's brother himself, was beyond Meg's comprehension. Judd or Robert never even compared their level of power to that of the Warden or his deputy, least of all a Warden with such high connections.

"Have you seen the Duke?"

"Seen him, yes. He's nothing impressive. Slight, if you ask me, when you see him out of armour, not tall and broad like his brother, from what I've heard of Edward. Not spoken to him though, so I cannot judge him there. I'm not expecting to be excited when I do. He'll be just the same as the rest, I'd wager. But as long as he doesn't interfere this far east, and keeps to his own borders, I'm sure we will get along perfectly well."

Meg hid her smile as Ben caught her eye, shaking his head subtly. "Sarah has prepared refreshment for you – for you all, I believe, from the work she was putting in. I'm sure she has thought of everything."

Alexander's face gave nothing away, however hard Meg searched. With a short nod, he gestured to the men as the horses were tied up for the day, and they marched into the bastle. Only Ben remained, as Meg placed a hand on his arm.

"What's the trouble out to the west? Anything that could harm Long Ridge?"

"No, just one of his tenants. There was a raid two nights ago, and they took five or so good cattle. However hard the man tried, nobody would support his trod."

"But you have to support a trod."

"Yes, but since Bridget died, fewer and fewer families are wanting anything to do with Gray. It's funny, don't repeat this, but I'm starting to think it was her who had the power around here."

Meg couldn't help but laugh. "Bridget? Power?"

"Not in the way you think. No control over Gray, or Henry, but I mean a quiet power. Perhaps respect would be a better word. Think how at Long Ridge, people listened to you or Hannah, just as much as they would to Robert or Judd. Or how many times they'll confide in you, rather than your brothers at all, and how you two have dealt with problems."

"Poor Bridget. All those years, keeping a calm head, probably keeping Alexander calmer than he would have been otherwise."

"I think so. And without that influence, well, I'm worried he'll get ahead of himself, and start seeing himself as more powerful than others will be happy about."

"He's already talking of the weakness of the Wardens," whispered Meg, glancing up to the hall level of the bastle, where she imagined Alexander was already acting the lord of the manor. "He frightens me."

"Is that why you sent Will away?"

Meg stared at him. "Cecily sent for him."

"No she didn't. Why would she? Tom's a capable man, and she would never do anything without checking with Robert first. So... If Cecily didn't ask for him, my next guess is that you sent him. I'm not sure I want to know why." Despite his words, Ben's raised eyebrows indicated that he was keen to know Meg's reason.

"I was scared for him. You're different, you're like a brother to me, but Will…"

"Oh no – not a romance? I could see there was an attraction there, but not an actual romance."

Meg suddenly found her feet endlessly interesting.

"Meg?"

"You cannot say anything!"

"And risk my own neck? Not a chance. But you did the right thing. Oh, Meg, you soft thing. Come on, let's go and get some food. Sarah's soups are legendary."

"You know she's his mistress?"

Ben stopped. "You know you can't really comment on that? And actually, you do know how dangerous it is, to even consider an affair yourself?"

"Well, it's over, isn't it?"

"Is it?"

Meg glanced at the horizon. "He's gone, so yes, it's over. Let's eat." She turned away, into the bastle. Whatever happened, there was no chance whatsoever of her confessing the full truth to Ben.

Not just yet. But her friend didn't look as convinced as she would have liked.

CHAPTER FIFTY-THREE

Will was waiting nervously at the edge of Long Ridge village, desperately searching the horizon for any hint of movement. He felt more anxious now than when he knew for a fact that a troop of raiders were heading his way. Hannah had been sure this was the morning they were expecting Ben, with the latest news from Cliffside, and instructions (which would, of course, as always be worded as an invitation) for Robert, Judd and their entourage to join Alexander and Cliffside in a raid over the border. He had seen the brothers' eyes darkening with every letter Ben delivered, and yet, for some reason, nothing had changed. This time there had been rumours of a kidnapping on the lands controlled by Gray in the last couple of days, and they were certain a summons would be arriving soon.

After what felt like an eternity, the lone figure emerged over the hill and began the ride towards the village, dust thrown up in its wake.

"Ben!" Will couldn't hide the relief in his voice at the sight of his friend.

For a moment, Ben didn't speak, just shook his head. "You're a fool."

"What? Why? What's happened? Is Meg—"

"Meg is fine. And I'll tell you that, because you are my friend, but I'll also tell you this – you need to forget her."

Will considered denying he knew what Ben was talking about, but knew it was hopeless. "I love her," he said, shrugging his shoulders.

"It doesn't matter. She isn't yours to love. She wasn't when she was here, and she certainly isn't now she belongs to Gray. So, as a friend, listen to me. Be loyal, defend her honour, be the best in every raid you can be, but don't go anywhere near her. Gray's getting dangerous, more so every week, and if he has the slightest reason to doubt her…"

***

"Has he harmed her?" Will asked.

"No," Ben lied, conveniently forgetting the cut arm Meg had been nursing that morning, from yet another breakage in the hall. That had been an accident, of sorts, rather than deliberate on Gray's part. He had meant to break the bowl, not injure Meg, Ben thought, even as he condemned himself for such a twisted reading of events. "But I would worry for her safety if anything was to reach him. Who else knows?"

"Nobody. Well, perhaps Hannah and Judd have guessed. But they would never betray us."

"Keep it that way," Ben replied shortly, as Robert and Judd approached them.

"More from our friendly neighbour?" asked Robert, as Ben greeted them both, handing over his letter.

"The usual, I suspect. There's been rumours of Scots kidnapping some of his tenants to the west, and he wants retribution."

Judd shook his head. "He's asking too much. We agreed to joint raids, showing and sharing strength, but not to be at his beck and call whenever he wanted an issue sorting out. Will he even be joining us?"

Will scoffed. Gray had been absent from their last two 'joint' raids, having found himself an excellent reason to be elsewhere. Ben noticed that as Will caught Judd's eye, it was clear both men felt the same way about their neighbour.

Robert ignored them. "We'll be there, we'll support him. Tell him, if we're going west, then it would make sense for us to spend the night at Cliffside on our return. It will be a good opportunity to see Meg at the same time. It's been too many weeks since we saw her. All well with you, Judd?"

His brother nodded. "She must be showing by now; it will be good to see her blooming."

***

Will felt his heart contract. His child, on show for everyone, albeit not in his name. He would have to watch his behaviour every second, and ensure he gave nothing away that could endanger either of them.

Three days later, the men of Long Ridge rode along the track Ben had ridden back, carrying Robert's assent to Gray's plan. Whatever Will thought of the situation, he couldn't help but be thrilled to see his beloved Meg again. Whatever happened the following night, he would do his best to steal even a few moments with her. If Robert's grim attitude the last couple of days was anything to go on, it might be all he got for months to come.

***

Meg had been watching out for the party from Long Ridge, despite her vow to herself not to do so. Peering into the distance, she knew it was hopeless trying to pick out Will amongst the group.

"You'll be sorry to know, I'm sure, that I warned him to stay away from you." Ben's voice startled her.

"I cannot avoid him entirely, that would seem just as strange, don't you think?" she replied, attempting a smile.

"You won't be on your own with him, not for a single moment, not if I have anything to do with it."

Meg sighed. She knew Ben's actions were for her own good, and that what he was suggesting was in everyone's best interests, but it didn't mean she had to agree with it. "I will be careful at all times, I can assure you."

"Come on then, let's go and meet them."

Minutes later, Meg found herself lifted off her feet in her brother's strong arms. Robert's smile was always contagious, but it was Judd who swept her into the air, always the one refusing to adhere to the rules of society.

"Mathers, and Mathers, good of you to join us," Alexander's voice made the group turn as one. "We'll be riding out immediately after dusk, so make sure your men are ready. We'll be taking plenty of ammunition, and I want no pistols going awry in the dark – you can use the forge to clean your weapons and sharpen your blades. There'll be food served at midday."

"Morning, Gray. Are you well?" Robert had clearly chosen to ignore the orders, thereby forcing his ally into politeness, whether he liked it or not.

Alexander practically snarled. "That wretched Warden won't let things lie, if you must know. Keeps poking his nose into things which aren't his business. At least this evening, I know he's over in the east, so we are going west, to show the bloody Scots that they cannot come into my territory without retribution."

"I heard of the kidnapping – do you know where the victims are being kept?"

"Not a clue. It's been a couple of days, so they could be anywhere. We cannot risk trying to get them back this evening; we'll take our revenge, and see if we can get some decent cattle out of it."

"You're not going to try and get them back?" asked Judd, the disgust in his voice barely disguised.

"How can we? No, this evening is about taking things back. If we find them, we find them, if not, then we will see what happens next week. There's been no ransom demand, no threat of blackmail. Who knows what the kidnappers even want?"

Alexander's indifference to his tenants' plight sickened Meg. Her own brothers were hard men, and everyone knew how harsh life was in this area, but to not even try? That was not the Mathers way, and she wished it wasn't the Gray way either.

Amidst the confusion, she had almost missed Will,

standing in the middle of the pack of men, carefully not pushing himself forward or drawing attention to himself. Catching his eye, she risked exchanging the quickest of smiles with him, unable to do anything more, before Alexander called to her, reminding her of the work needed back at the bastle to prepare the meal for everyone. Not wanting to delay and risk an argument, she gave her brothers a final smile, noting with brief curiosity the winks being exchanged between them, before heading inside to where she knew Sarah was already working at preparing the food.

It was going to be a long, hard day.

CHAPTER FIFTY-FOUR

The horses were starting to tire as Cliffside finally came back into sight. One final surge and they would be in relative safety, providing the Wardens didn't work out which way they had travelled, and nobody had followed them. That thought wasn't one Will wanted to entertain.

Suddenly, Alexander was beside Will, their steeds so close together it would have been nothing for Will to slip the knife from his jacket and cut through the older man's bridle. In the dark, in all the confusion, would anyone really be able to spot the difference between wear and tear, and deliberate slicing? His hand began to leave his own reins, when he realised Robert was directly ahead of him. Will must have passed more of the gang than he thought as they raced through the night. If he was behind Robert, and beside Alexander, he was far too exposed to consider murder. Besides, at this speed, he could just as easily topple himself, and where would that leave him? He settled back in his saddle as they reached the edge of the village.

The women were waiting in the enclosure, waiting, as usual, to witness the raid's spoils and their homecoming. The men were greeted with open arms, as horses were secured and cattle counted. No hostages to worry about tonight, from either side. They had been lucky.

Meg was standing at the door to the bastle, in a cruel echo of where she had been standing that fateful night when all this began. Her eyes were scanning the scene, and Will knew she would be taking in every detail. Especially the location of her husband. The man in question was passing through the group, embracing each man in turn, loudly singing the praises of those from his own land over those from Long Ridge. But the longer he was congratulating himself, thought Will, the longer it was until he went anywhere near Meg. The thought alone made Will's skin crawl. He knew Alexander rarely troubled Meg in the evenings any more, but knowing that at least some of her nights were spent alongside the man was bad enough.

Judd ended up being the first man to approach his sister, being rewarded with a warm smile, her eyes still alert to their surroundings. She blinked as Alexander finally joined them, wrapping a territorial arm around his wife as they stood at the entrance of his bastle. Will's stomach tightened. He would never get over this jealousy, he thought, as he forced down both the bile rising in his throat, and the instinct to reach for his sword. If he couldn't kill the man whilst out raiding, he certainly couldn't do it now.

"An excellent return, I see, husband. You and the men are to be congratulated," said Meg, a forced smile on her lips. Will knew when she was acting. "Is everyone returned safely?"

"Everyone, yes, but we lost a horse. That lad of your brothers, Ben. Went flying, the idiot, could have lost us the advantage of surprise."

"Ben? Is he harmed?" Finally, she turned to Will. "Did you see what happened?"

"His horse lost its footing, that's all, and he hit the ground hard. But he's winded, nothing more, and sleeping it off now. He'll be back to normal the day after tomorrow. You know how he is."

"But where is he? I'll go to him, if you don't mind, Alexander?" Meg turned to her husband, who responded with nothing more than a shrug. Taking it as consent, she nodded to Will. "Is he at the forge? We'll go there now."

Seeing the sparkle in her eye, Will was glad Ben had suffered nothing more than a couple of bruises and a wounded pride. Watching Meg rush back inside to collect the bag of herbs, he started to plan the glorious hour they would have together whilst she was apparently healing

Ben, who would no doubt be asleep in his bed by now, and none the wiser as to what was going on in the main room of the cottage. It had been torture for Will, knowing that he was so close to Meg and their child – his child – but unable to do anything about it. He was lucky it wasn't his own horse which had tumbled, the way his mind had kept wandering, but somehow, he had stayed upright, and poor Ben had gone over. At least this would give them the briefest of moments, before they would both need to be back in the bastle, and Alexander reclaimed his wife.

"Ready?"

He hadn't even noticed her emerge from the door, stopping to tell Judd and Robert where she was going. That twinkle was back in her eye, as he nodded and led the way back to the forge's cottage.

As soon as the door slammed shut behind them, Will spun on his heel, took Meg in his arms and kissed her, not stopping to check whether Ben truly was asleep.

"I've missed you," he gasped, resisting the urge to unlace her dress.

"I'm so glad you're safe," she replied, pushing him away from her for a moment, and looking into his eyes. "You are safe?"

"Completely, see." He turned around slowly, full of joy just to be in her presence again.

The joy for both of them was to be short-lived, as a blood-curdling cry shocked them both, causing Ben to jolt through the door from the other room.

"What the hell was that?" he cried, not even pausing to question or admonish the two lovers as they jumped apart at the sight of him.

Meg went to open the door, before Will pulled her back.

"No. Don't you even think about going out there until we know what's happening. For once, you're going to do exactly as I tell you."

Without giving her a chance to argue, he ordered her

through to the backroom of the cottage, thrusting an axe into her hands. "Use it if anything happens, anything at all – we all know you can handle it well enough."

He gave her a swift kiss, then he and Ben moved to stand either side of the tiny window at the front of the room.

CHAPTER FIFTY-FIVE

The sight which met them was horrifying. A gang of men, bigger than any that either of the young men had previously encountered on a single raid, was tearing their way through the village towards the bastle.

"We need to warn Robert and Judd," whispered Ben, urgently.

"No need. Look," replied Will, pointing to where the men of the bastle had come out to meet the raiders, weapons at the ready. "Still, we cannot hide in here. Come on."

Keeping out of sight, they crept out via the forge itself, swords in hand, having spent the ammunition from their pistols on the raid.

"Who are they?" hissed Will. "English or Scot?"

"I cannot see from this angle, but I'm going with unfriendly, either way. Who knows, when you think who Gray has offended or raided this last few months?"

They stayed in the shadows as best they could, taking advantage of the moonless night, and their knowledge of their new home, gradually gathering a handful of others who had also returned to their homes, rather than going to the bastle to celebrate the raid with their master, including John, uneasy at spending any longer than necessary in Gray's company since his beating. Their progress was marked by the sound of cries from the bastle, as both parties loosed arrows in the direction of their enemy, as well as throwing bricks and sharpened stones, kept for such an event within the enclosure. Will prayed Meg would be safe where they had left her, and that Robert, Judd and the other Long Ridge men would be secure within the bastle. As things stood, their small group, and the residents within their cottages, were the ones at risk, but they all knew that running would never be a viable option against these men on their horses.

"If we go round to the back entrance of the enclosure, we'll be able to add our number to the defenders," whispered Will urgently, finding himself at the front of the group, leading the way.

The others nodded, weapons primed. As one, they wound their way through the shadows, keeping as low to the ground as possible to avoid any risk of being seen through the cottages' small windows, as the raiders headed towards the bastle, ransacking along the way. All the men had come out now, firing what weapons they could as their enemy approached.

Will looked desperately at the group, praying that Meg had remained safely inside the forge. But he had a feeling she wouldn't sit quietly and allow her brothers, and men she had known from childhood, stand an attack like this without doing something to try and help them. Suddenly he saw the women. They had gathered at the top of the bastle, some even out on the tower's roof, brandishing whatever weapons they could find.

As their small group reached the bastle, they heard gunshots, cries, and the clash of metal on metal. The two groups had come together just outside the enclosure, Alexander and Robert each forcing their way into the heart of the battle, slashing through the raiders with their blades, screaming orders at their men. Behind Robert, Will saw Judd, loyal as always, right where his brother needed him, watching everything, and counter-commanding as needed. The two were a perfect team. The Cliffside men were less organised, but more ruthless – Will had noticed this over their times riding out together. Now it was even more evident, as they charged forward, roaring for blood from the men who dared invade their homes. It didn't matter that just hours earlier, Cliffside and Long Ridge men had been guilty of the very same act. This was their home, and they would defend it to the end.

Some of the raiders had started firing arrows up at the

bastle now, hoping to cut through some of the narrow arrow-slits, or hit one of the rooftop defenders. Will caught his breath for a second as he heard a woman's scream, or at least thought he did; he knew the men could be just as terrified when injured in the heat of a battle.

Suddenly John jumped on him, shoving both of them out the way of a passing bolt. They had been seen. It grazed the arm of the man behind them, but they surged on, their immediate plan being to make what rear-guard action they could, rounding on the attackers whilst their own men kept them occupied at the front.

It was more violent than anything Will had encountered in his life, and that included having been on the receiving end of one of Gray's attacks as a child. The man's anger and cruelty hadn't diminished as he aged, and (as anyone might have expected) what he gave out, others were more than willing to give back in return. Now, steel clashed on steel, the sound and smell of pistols firing filled the air, and Will was sure it wasn't just in his imagination that he could sense the metallic tang of blood. They were all exhausted already, there was no way all of them could come through this; he just hoped that he, Ben and the Mathers siblings could make it.

For a horrid, heartless moment, he didn't care whether they were the only ones left alive at the end, as long as they were alive. He wanted to run back to the forge and stand guard at the cottage door until it was all over, but he knew that was the best way to ensure Meg wouldn't be safe. At least the way things were, any attackers in that part of the village would assume, having seen him and Ben leave, that the cottage was left empty. It was the only thought he could rely on at the moment.

The fighting intensified, until finally he caught a glimpse of the man leading their attackers. Elliot. Then he saw it. The raiders were being remarkably selective in their violence, only truly going for the Cliffside men, whereas the Long Ridge men all seemed to be on the periphery.

They were fighting, yes, but it was more akin to how he and Ben were when they were practising a new skill they had picked up. He had assumed it was luck that he and Ben had made it to the bastle unscathed, whilst three of the men in their party had fallen, albeit only with minor injuries. Without another moment, he pulled on Ben's arm, drawing him into a doorway.

"Ben. It's the Elliots. Look at them. Really look at them."

"Look at them? Have you gone mad? Throw things at them, fire at them, but don't look at them!"

"No, man, I mean it – LOOK! Watch the fighting."

He watched as the one-sided, almost staged nature of the fight dawned in his friend's eyes.

"But, but we're still fighting them. Aren't we?"

"I thought we were, but maybe not."

They watched until Robert and Judd came back into view. "It looks like they're back on the training yard," whispered Ben, turning to Will. "What's going on?"

Will shook his head. "Perhaps all that blackmail money paid off? Honestly, I have no idea, but whatever it is, we missed the start, and if the Elliots see us with this lot, they might think we're mixed up in it more than we are. Come on, let's get back to the forge, and stay out of sight until it's over." The action felt cowardly, leaving his fellow-villagers in potential danger, but it was true: neither of the young men had any clue what was happening, and the last thing Will wanted was to drag him and Ben into a battle they didn't know the meaning behind, or which side they ought to be fighting on.

Silently, with the grace of dancers, they slipped back into the shadows. They would have made it in a matter of moments, if an almighty roar hadn't brought everything to a shuddering halt.

Alexander Gray was racing out of the bastle like a man possessed, eyes wide, a pistol in each hand, charging directly towards Elliot.

CHAPTER FIFTY-SIX

"I will kill you! I will kill you!" The raw fury in Gray's voice was enough to shake even the most hardened reiver.

Seeing his enemy rushing at him, Elliot's obvious desire for self-preservation won out over his courage. Reaching for the metal dish that had landed at his feet just moments before, he threw it, spinning through the air, directly at Gray's head, forcing him to raise an arm in his own protection. It was only a moment, but it was enough for Elliot to be out of the enclosure and halfway to the protection of the nearest cottage, with his men already forming a guard around him. One of the most feared reivers and blackmailers in the region was not going to lose his life that night. Gray attempted to chase them down, but even his own men were standing dumbfounded, and didn't react quickly enough.

As the last of Elliot's men rushed back into the darkness, following their leader, it was almost as though nothing had happened. Gray had never lost his temper in the heat of battle before. It was at the heart of the action, Will had noticed, that Gray was at his coolest, keeping his head together, aware of tactics at every stage. Now, as they watched him racing into the night, on his own, still screaming at the top of his voice, they wondered what on earth could have happened to cause such a change in him.

It was Hal who revealed their answer, as he staggered out of the bastle with blood pouring from a wound above his eye, calling for Meg.

"Where is she? She's needed. Please."

"I'm here," Meg's voice cut through the men's mumblings, as she hurried back into her home, carrying the bag she had taken with her such a short time earlier. She exchanged the briefest of glances with Will and Ben, before vanishing into the bastle and up the stairs.

***

The sight which confronted her in the upper chamber brought her to a halt. Now she understood Alexander's anguish. Sarah was lying, pale and still, in the middle of the floor, a pool of blood slowly spreading beneath her head. A blood-stained rock lay on the floor just feet away, surrounded by shards of broken glass. Meg could see at once that the woman was beyond saving, and might even be dead already, but nonetheless sank to her knees beside her, knowing she had to try.

"Sarah? Sarah, can you hear me?" Nothing. "Sarah! Look at me!" There was tiniest flutter of eyelids, but it wasn't enough. Sarah's skin was already cooling fast, and as Meg looked on in horror, the saw the muscles in her former rival's face relax for the final time. Aware that there was now a crowd of men behind her, including Robert, Judd, Hal and Will, Meg shifted Sarah into a more dignified position, then rose, and shook her head at the men. "There was never going to be anything I could do."

"What will he say?" There was no mistaking who Hal was referring to.

The silence was deafening, as Meg felt the blood pounding in her head. There was only one person Alexander would blame for this. First Henry, now Sarah; how many more crises could he set at her door?

Robert was the first to move, reaching for her hand. "Come on, Meg, we can go. You shouldn't be here when he gets back."

Meg was frozen in shock, her feet refusing to move, however hard her mind tried to tell them that Robert was right, that this was her chance to flee. Too late, the message reached her legs. As she tried to turn, Alexander reappeared in the doorway.

He didn't even look at Sarah's body, instead scanning the faces of everyone in the room. Only Meg had the courage to meet his gaze.

"There was nothing I could do."

Alexander was just inches from her now, his eyes cold, dark and empty, pools of anger, close to brimming over.

"I know you hated her, but this?" He continued before she had the chance to defend herself. "Well, be aware, that she leaves a very big hole here at Cliffside, one I expect you to make much more of an effort to fill."

"I hope that isn't a threat, Gray." Judd's voice was surprisingly calm. Only Meg and Robert would have heard the icy chill hidden beneath and recognise the sinister undertone.

"A threat? But of course not, my dear brother. Merely an observation. A sincere one." This last was directed once again at Meg. There was still no warmth to his tone. "Clear this room by the time I return," he ordered, before gesturing to John to follow him. "And I want no outsiders to be here when I return. Cliffside shall be in mourning. Again." Without a backward glance, he was gone.

Meg saw the nervous glances exchanged by Robert and Judd.

"You should go," she said, forcing her voice under control. "Nobody will return here tonight, but Long Ridge may need defending." She had seen the Elliots, and knew that Long Ridge would be safe, but she needed her brothers to leave, and to take Will with them. Cliffside was even more dangerous a place for him now. She turned away, unable to look at any of them. Only a squeeze of her hand made her look back.

"You know where we are lass, you know where we are." The affection had returned to Judd's voice, as he forced a smile, before the Long Ridge men filed out of the room. Only Will looked as though he might try and argue, until Ben moved to stand between him and Meg, forcing Will's hand.

She couldn't bring herself to watch them leave. She feared that, if she did, her resolve would crumble, and she would let them carry her away, home to Long Ridge. She couldn't let it happen. Gray would see it as kidnap, even theft, and they all knew all too well what happened to those who stole from Alexander Gray.

In silence, Meg knelt beside Sarah's body. Using the cloth the poor woman had been carrying, she tried make her more presentable. She would have to change the dress later, and clean the floor, she thought.

Only Hal, of the men, approached her. "I'll take her to the cottage," he said, moving to lift Sarah from the floor, casting a sorrowful glance towards the poor woman's father, who was sobbing silently in the corner.

"No," said Meg. "Take her to Henry's old bedchamber. She, at least, meant a lot to Alexander. She should be here."

Meg felt her eyes filling with tears as the woman she had seen as a rival since her first morning at Cliffside lay still in Hal's arms. Was Alexander's affection really something worth fighting over? It was too late now to think about what might have been, if they had worked together, rather than against each other. Her eyes fell on Claire, loitering as though waiting for instruction. Would she be Sarah's replacement, Meg wondered, or would Alexander mean it when he said she would be made to fill the gap Sarah left? Meg wasn't sure which option filled her with more dread.

It was over a week before Alexander would allow Sarah's body to be removed from the bastle. Not even the protests of her father moved him, until the priest joined his voice to the cry.

The funeral was quiet. Meg was banned from attending, not that she relished the thought of being there. She prepared a meal for when they returned from church, carefully avoiding anything Sarah had taken pride in making. It wasn't much of a gesture, but it was the only way forward she could think of. As the night drew in, she retired as early as she could, slipping away and curling up as tight as she could on the great bed in their chamber.

The baby was giving her some protection from his attention, but she knew that as soon as the child was born, he would return to her bed, out of spite if nothing else. She was sure there was no attraction or affection in it, if the arguments over the past few days were any indication. Meg was in the wrong whatever she did. If she said nothing, she was too quiet and sullen, but if she dared open her mouth, he criticised every opinion she raised. She knew the men were beginning to feel sorry for her, with even Sarah's father being noticeably softer towards her, finding reason after reason for Meg to visit him in his cottage at the far end of the village. Despite the subtle efforts of almost everyone in the village, Alexander's seemingly unrivalled hatred of Meg was growing with every passing day. She knew it had to come to a head, and the thought of it was beginning to scare her.

CHAPTER FIFTY-SEVEN

The next morning had started badly, as Alexander crashed, still half-drunk, into their chamber, demanding Meg move so that he could inspect the ammunition store. Sensing danger, and wanting him nowhere near the powder in his state, she had managed to manoeuvre him back into the main room of their private quarters, before calling for Katherine to fetch Hal. Since Sarah's death, Katherine was the only woman who had dared spend any longer than necessary in the bastle, her position as Gray's illegitimate daughter giving her at least that protection from the man. Meg wondered who the girl's mother was, and whether she was even still in the village. She had never seen Katherine with anyone; it was just as likely her mother had been one of Alexander's Hexham conquests.

Hal approached the chamber warily, carrying the bread and cheese Katherine must have forced into his hands, in an attempt to sober Gray up as quickly as possible. But Meg could see her husband was in no mood for seeing sense.

"You should eat, husband, keep your strength up," she said, forcing a smile into her voice.

"Why? What do you know? Who have you been listening to?" His words were half-slurred, half-growled.

"Nobody, I just mean, it's best to stay on your guard, with your wits about you."

"My 'wits' are perfectly well about me, thank you very much!" His voice was sharper now, the anger forcing the drunkenness from his tone. "Stop being so bloody patronising, 'Saint Margaret'. A little ale and wine never hurt anyone."

"Hardly fitting behaviour to allow your men to see you in such a state." The words were out of her mouth before she could stop herself.

"What did you say?" Alexander didn't even raise his voice, but Meg's blood ran cold at the darkness of his tone.

"I didn't mean, Alexander, please—"

"No, please, continue. Do let me know, as always, how inferior I am in comparison to your saintly brothers and their courageous band of warriors. I don't know why we bother even trying, or why you bother wasting your time on us, when everything is clearly so much better back at your precious Long Ridge." He sneered at her. "Why don't you just go back, and be done with it?"

Without a moment's hesitation, she hurried across the room, stopping just inches from him.

"Because you are my husband, and the father of my child, and my place is here." The mention of the child had worked before, and she prayed it would calm him now. "Alexander!" She forced him to look her in the eye.

"What?"

Her mind froze. "I…"

"Pathetic," he snarled. "You finally get my attention, and you have nothing to say. I hope this doesn't happen when your adored siblings ask for you so-renowned advice. Perhaps they are more efficient now you've left them alone; they can actually get a decision made. I always have thought them a little too cowed in their thought processes, lacking any direction. Pathetic," he repeated, "to be so controlled by a woman. No wonder neither of them has ever taken a wife – I doubt you would have allowed it."

A flash of red fury blinded her. How dare he bring her brothers into their petty argument? To her frustration, the words still wouldn't come, but she felt her hands balling into fists, and before she could stop herself, they were rising from her sides.

Then he laughed. If he hadn't laughed, everything might have been well.

"You would dare strike me? Do not be ridiculous!"

In a heartbeat, he lurched forward, grabbing both her wrists in his larger hands, and pinning them to her sides as they both ended up staggering towards the rail at the top of the steps.

"Let go of me!" she screamed, finally finding her voice, and wanting his hands anywhere but on her at that moment.

As she wriggled to try and free herself of Alexander's grasp, he pushed her away. His face was flushed dark, his eyes full of cold anger.

Meg realised a moment too late that with the force she was approaching the railing, it wouldn't hold her weight. Time moved with sickening slowness, as the wood cracked, and she fell through the gap, down onto the wooden steps below. The top two took the brunt of her fall, as her skirts wrapped around her legs and arms, entangling her and preventing her from reaching out and stopping the inevitable. The world spun on her axis as she half-rolled, half-fell the rest of the distance before landing with a dull thud on the stone floor below.

It felt like an eternity before Meg was able to open her eyes. She was aware of footsteps approaching on all sides, as well as the heavy tread of Alexander's boots on the stairs. Slowly she flexed each finger, each arm, each leg: nothing seemed broken. It was only as the shock began to wear off, that she was aware of the cramps in her stomach. Closing her eyes in hope, she focused on each shallow, ragged breath, hoping against hope that it was just the jolting of the fall that had made her feel nauseous. She forced her legs tight together, as though she would keep the baby from harm within her, as she felt a damp warmth spread through her skirts.

Alexander's strong grip was a surprise as he arrived at the bottom of the stairs and reached down to her, sweeping her up into a seating position, leaning against the wall.

"Meg, Meg, look at me!"

She squinted through the tears which were starting to fill her eyes, at the realisation of what might be happening as the pain inside her grew stronger. The last thing she wanted to do was look at Alexander. Instead, she scanned the room, until she at last found the face she was looking for.

Ben.

His face was a picture of shock, as he watched the girl he had known since they were children slump in distraught agony.

"Go," she half-whispered, half-cried at him, hoping he would understand instinctively what she meant.

She watched as he wiped his face with his hands, then physically pulled himself upright. He gave her a barely perceptible nod at her, then turned on his heel and rushed out of the building.

The sound of hooves followed soon after, as Alexander was distracted, trying to encourage Meg to her feet. Half-aware of the need to keep him that way, Meg forced herself to look up at him, keeping his attention just long enough for her loyal servant to be out of the village and racing as fast as he could back to Long Ridge.

CHAPTER FIFTY-EIGHT

Will was bored. After a morning practising with Tom and testing the weight of a new sword, he was now sitting, pretending to polish the blade, but in reality looking out over the village from Meg's favourite rock, enjoying the late afternoon sunshine, and wishing something would happen to take his mind off missing her. It was pathetic, he thought, acting no better than one of the soft-headed (and soft-hearted) lads you saw following the finer ladies around on market day, their eyes practically popping out of their heads whenever a smile was thrown their way. It was far deeper for him and Meg. She was carrying his child, for Heaven's sake, a child to which he could only ever be a guide, a mentor. Not even an uncle, he thought, kicking a stone away from his foot in anger.

He was so distracted that he didn't notice the sound of the horse approaching until it was almost upon him.

"Will! Will! Where are they?" Ben's voice drew his attention.

"What? Why?·The bastle. What's happened?"

Ben was gone without another word. Will chased after the horse, now slowed to a trot, but Ben showed no signs of reducing the pace any further. They reached the enclosure at the same time, Ben throwing the reins at one of the lads playing in the dust.

"Robert! Judd!" he bellowed, as he rushed into the lower level of the bastle and up the stairs, taking them two at a time.

The brothers rushed to greet him at the top of the steps, before pushing him towards a chair, which he collapsed into, trying to catch his breath. By the time Ben had finished speaking, Will could feel the blood running hot in his veins.

"The baby?" he demanded, not caring now whether

Robert or Judd found cause to wonder why he was asking.

Ben shook his head. "I don't know. There… there was blood. Meg was in such a state, I couldn't tell how bad it was, but it could be the worst."

Will watched the brothers turn pale, then glance at each other.

"Well?" he shouted again. "What are you going to do?"

He saw the hesitation in their eyes. They paused just half a moment too long for his liking.

"If you won't go and rescue her and bring her back here, then I will – with or without your help." He was already making his way to the weapons store, tightening his sword belt as he went.

"Will, come on lad. Of course we'll go, but we need to think about this—" Robert began, until Judd raised his hand, cutting him off.

"The child… It's yours, isn't it?"

Will froze, his hand on the lid of the chest. What was his punishment likely to be, he wondered, for stealing the virtue of his masters' sister? Then he realised he didn't care.

"Yes," he said, continuing to open the lid, and reaching inside for two pistols, and a second, smaller sword to fix to his belt. "And I love her, and she loves me, and if you don't come with me now, and help me kill the bastard who may well have killed our child, your nephew, then that's your choice. But I'm leaving, and leaving now."

He turned to go down the stairs, still not looking back at any of them. He wanted neither their pity nor fury. The bulk of Judd blocking his path pulled him up short.

"You're not going alone. But neither are you going now. It'll not be long, but we're taking every man we can muster, and you are going to wait for that to happen. Robert," he called over his shoulder, "gather every weapon we have, whilst I get the men."

Robert didn't meet Will's eye as he walked past him to retrieve the rest of the arms from their store. "You love her?"

"Yes Sir."

"Then let's go and save her."

Will paced as he watched the others shrug into their padded jackets, pull on their breastplates, and prime their weapons. They had done this hundreds of times, in practice and in anger; he couldn't understand what was taking them so long this time. He went to shout, only for Judd to hold him back.

"They'll be ready when they're ready, lad. You don't want this to be the time they rush and forget something in their haste, do you?"

Will almost turned away, not trusting himself to respond in a fitting manner, then saw the dark determination on Judd's face. Meg wasn't being abandoned in their time-taking; Meg was being saved by their taking care. "Still, we need to be on our way as soon as possible."

Finally, Robert gave the sign that the men were ready to leave. Even then, as they left Long Ridge behind, the bastle a flurry of activity as Hannah and the other women readied themselves for Meg's return, it felt to Will as though their horses were barely moving above a trot. He looked over at Robert.

"We need to go harder, Sir, along the direct path. Why are you leading us through the woods?"

Robert shook his head. "Tactics, lad. Don't think I'm not furious, but that's the difference: we need to be clever as well as angry. By now Gray will likely have sent a party to intercept us, don't you agree?"

Will cursed his own stupidity. He would have used the direct track, and ridden into whatever trap Gray had set for them. For he would surely have sent somebody by now, as soon as he realised Ben was gone. Just as Robert was right to ensure his men were properly equipped, he was also right about this. Will still had a lot to learn if he was ever going to be in his master's position.

They were pushing the horses hard, more than they would in any raid. Will could feel that now, but then, this time the prize was even greater: the safety of their darling Meg. Will could see it in the men's faces – this was one battle they were not prepared to lose.

***

At Cliffside, Meg knew the old woman, Elspeth, was pushing against her stomach, trying to determine whether or not the child could be saved, but she couldn't feel her touch. She was frozen, numb, held between feelings of agony and emptiness, trying to cling to the tiny fragment of hope, that she hadn't actually felt anything come away, nor seen the great flood of blood she would have expected if the worst had already happened. She knew the child was struggling; she didn't need Elspeth's expertise to deduce that, but she was willing it to hold on. This was her only connection with Will, but not just that – it was also the only reason Alexander had for bothering to maintain the pretence of their marriage. Meg knew he had never loved her, perhaps not even liked her that much. But now he actively hated her, and with no child to keep her safe... Even in the midst of her numbness, she was sure there would no longer be anything other than danger for her at Cliffside.

CHAPTER FIFTY-NINE

The tall tower of Gray's home finally came into view, but it only served to heighten the quickening of Will's pulse. He couldn't deny that he was anxious about what lay ahead. There was going to be one hell of a confrontation; that much was obvious to all. He watched as Gray himself walked out of the main doorway and into the sunlight. Without a moment's hesitation, Will reached for his sword, but Robert cut in front of him, blocking his path.

"You follow orders here, don't forget that." Robert's tone was blunt, and he looked down on Will, taking advantage of their difference in height.

Will didn't move his hand.

"Gentlemen, this is unexpected. I'm afraid my wife is ill, and unable to receive visitors, even family, so you'll find this a wasted journey. I must ask you to leave." Gray was charming, almost seductive, with the confidence of a man used to getting his own way.

Robert smiled as he dismounted, gesturing to the others to follow suit. Will could tell he was now hiding his earlier anger, spreading his arms wide in greeting.

"Some ale and refreshment first, surely? And if she is ill, even more cause for us to see our sister, wouldn't you agree?"

Will saw a fleeting glimmer of panic cross Gray's face, as the man cast his eye over the size the brothers' entourage, and evidently spotted Ben amongst the pack. The poor man was exhausted, but had insisted on returning to help Meg.

"I really do think—" Gray started.

"Will!" Meg's cry from an upper window drew everyone's attention. She had pulled herself up to the window, and was looking down on events.

"Meg! I'm coming for you, we're all coming for you!"

Will pulled his sword from its sheath and rushed towards the door. They wouldn't stop him this time. To his relief, the brothers were just inches behind him in their reaction.

The clash of steel on steel reverberated, as Gray yelled to his men, drawing his own weapon to meet Judd's, as Robert swerved past him, knocking John and two others off their feet.

Will took the stairs to the main floor two at a time, only to hear the heavy thud of a trapdoor closing above his head. Whoever was with Meg had somehow got her up to the top floor, and didn't want her being reached.

"We're close, Meg, we're coming," he shouted up to her, half-wanting a reply, but knowing she needed to keep all the strength she could muster. He couldn't lose her – not now, not like this.

With no other option available, he turned to go down, only to find Gray blocking his path.

"Get out of my property, now, or I will have no issue running you through, believe me."

"Oh, I do believe you, don't you worry. But you don't scare me, not this time. You don't remember me, do you?"

Gray paused, as though amused by the distraction Will might afford him before he died. Then he shrugged. "Why would I? You're no more than a child."

Will shook his head. He knew he was wasting time, but he needed Gray to know this. Whether he was about to kill Gray, or he was about to die at Gray's hand, it needed saying.

"Yes, that's right. I was a child when you tore through our village, burned our homes and killed my parents. But it's pointless asking you if you remember, isn't it? Just another village, another set of lives destroyed. We had just been attacked, days before. We heard you were coming, and we thought you were coming to help us, to try and take back what had been stolen. But no, you were coming to take advantage of a weakened community, and ended up stealing what the first lot hadn't been able to carry. You are the lowest of the low, Alexander Gray. It will be a pleasure to send you to Hell." As the words tumbled out, Will took the briefest moment of pleasure at the look of surprise on Gray's face.

Will smiled. He was braced now, his sword solid in his hand, as he advanced on Gray. His blood was pounding, but he was almost excited. Win or lose, he was doing his best to avenge everyone he had ever loved.

Robert was at the top of the stairs, with Judd just behind him. Will had last seen Ben vanishing around the side of the bastle. The rest of the men stayed in the lower level, keeping Gray's men from reaching their master, and they had the edge so far. Will knew that whatever happened to him, the brothers would be upon Gray in moments, and finish whatever he had started. They would rescue Meg too. The thought gave him at least some comfort.

He felt, as much as heard, the roar from Gray, as the older man rushed towards him, sword aloft, but he didn't have Will's agility. As he had told Meg, all those years being taught to dance had made him quick on his feet. With perfect timing, he swung out of Gray's way, causing him to falter as he tried to turn before colliding with the table, pushed against the wall in the commotion of getting Meg up to the top floor. By the time he was recovered, Will was at his back, bringing his sword down on Gray's arm, slashing the fine material, and connecting with flesh beneath.

Gray's curses proved that Will had hit his mark. But it wasn't enough. The lust for revenge in Will had gone far beyond being satisfied by just wounding Gray and taking back his beloved Meg. This had to be to the death.

CHAPTER SIXTY

Gray was staggering now, but the injured arm was his left, not his sword arm. Holding the bleeding arm next to his body, he lumbered towards Will, the sword in his right hand as steady as he could manage. He slashed the metal towards Will's sword arm, clearly trying to take out the younger man and weaken him enough for the kill. But Will was faster, and fuelled by fury. Again and again he defended himself against Gray's weakening strikes, until at last he hit his mark: a body blow, not enough to kill, but enough to knock the energy out of him. Will watched as Gray fell forward onto his knees, spittle tainted with blood as he exclaimed with pain.

The moment Gray hit the floor, the trapdoor to the upper level was pulled back.

"Will!"

Ben's voice, rather than Meg's, shocked Will into looking up for a moment; his friend must have used the external wooden stairs to find another way in, in case his sword was needed. He returned his gaze to his own floor just in time to prevent a half-hearted attempt by Gray to reach for his sword. Will pressed his foot against the man's wrist, and shook his head.

"I don't think so. This is for my parents, for Bridget, for Henry, for every person you have ever, ever hurt – and most of all, for my child." He grinned at the confusion on Gray's face. "Yes, I didn't mention that before, did I? Meg was mine before she was yours, and the child was only ever mine."

He raised his sword.

"No!"

A second voice came from the upper chamber. Katherine, this time, not Ben, with a lit candle in her hand.

"Drop your sword," she said, sounding calmer than she

looked, stains from Meg's gown covering her own, her hair slick with sweat. "Drop your sword, or I send us all where you want to send him." She gestured with the candle.

"A candle? Why should I fear one candle?"

"The powder, Will. The main bed's the ammunition store." Meg's voice was weak, and Will couldn't see her, but he could hear the fear in her words.

"The bed?" He turned back to stare at Gray. "You have been making my Meg, and my child, sleep above an ammunition store?"

"I'll set it alight, I swear I'll do it."

"No, you won't. She won't." Ben reappeared above the trapdoor, wrenched the candle out of Katherine's hand and pulled her away, out of sight.

Will nodded, relief flooding through him. With one final thrust of his sword, it was all over. Without even stopping to look at Gray's body, Will was scrambling up onto a chair, hauling himself through the open trapdoor to Meg.

***

At Gray's death, Katherine's screams seemed as though they would split the very fabric of the building; he had been her father, after all. As Ben tried to comfort her, Robert and Judd rushed down to the lower floor, dreading the reaction of the Cliffside men. To Judd's surprise, the swords were still as they descended. The two groups of men were standing, if not quite together, certainly not at war. Hal stepped forward.

"They told us. What the master had done, I mean. He said she was ill, that she'd threatened to kill him, that she had betrayed us to you, in some sick revenge. We didn't know about the fall, or the risk to the child. We swear, we didn't know what he had done."

Robert eyed the man carefully. Swords were still drawn; this was no peace yet. "He's dead."

Hal nodded. "Then what do you propose happens now?"

"To us?"

"To us. And to Cliffside. We cannot afford any trouble from this. Easier for everyone if Gray's death goes down as simply one of those things. These are dangerous lands. A reiver's life isn't always a long one."

Judd looked at the men surrounding his brother and himself. Could it be an elaborate trap, set to ensnare them all? Was Gray even truly dead?

It was as though Hal could read his thoughts. "It's no trap. I can speak for us all. Your sister's been good to us, despite his treatment of her. This is her home, if she were to insist on her rights. There are no other legitimate children." He was choosing his words carefully.

Judd nodded. "It isn't our decision. You'll have to speak to Meg."

Hal nodded, and made his way into the bastle.

***

Meg felt herself trembling as Hal entered the chamber she had used as her private quarters since her arrival. With the powder still so readily available, she didn't want to meet him in the main bedchamber. She listened as he outlined his proposal, forcing herself to be calm, her hands clasped in hope and protection over her stomach. There had still been no further blood loss.

"You would choose me?" she asked, looking at him as evenly as she could manage.

"We've heard of the advice you've given your brothers. We know you could run this land well," Hal replied, taking a step towards, and eyeing Will as though noticing him for the first time. "And if you had retainers from Long Ridge, then, perhaps we could still look to work together. For the benefit of all of us."

"I won't be having any retainers from Long Ridge,"

Meg replied, feeling her strength return, despite the pain still rushing through her. "In a few months, I will have a husband from Long Ridge, and if you cannot accept him, then I want to know now, and we will leave without another word being spoken." She was hoping her gamble would pay off: that Hal would realise how suspicious it would look if both husband and wife were to be replaced. If she stayed, as Gray's widow, then there could be at least some semblance of a normal transition from Gray's ownership to the next. After all, there was no other family on Gray's side.

Hal's widening eyes told her he finally realised what she meant. "This young thing?" he asked, nodding to Will.

Meg smiled. "This young thing indeed. Will you accept him?"

Hal seemed to mull it over for a moment, then nodded. "Aye, we'll accept him."

Will stepped forward, as the two men shook hands.

Meg smiled. Perhaps it could be well after all.

As though to confirm her thoughts, she felt the tiniest movement inside her stomach.

EPILOGUE

Meg couldn't help but laugh as the rain lashed against the bastle's window, drawing her from a fitful, restless sleep. At least it was no longer the risk of explosion that was keeping her awake at night, since Cliffside's gunpowder and ammunition had been safely removed to an outbuilding. The weather had been perfect for her first, heart-breaking wedding; it was only fitting that today, as she married the love of her life, the weather was horrendous. A cry from her former chamber pulled her from the final moments of drowsiness, as she hurried through to tend to little Henry. Named after the man who would have been an uncle, of sorts, the baby had somehow been accepted by the people of Cliffside, and he was doted on more than Meg could ever have imagined.

Later, as Lizzie and Hannah helped her dress, they chattered about the lifetime of happiness which lay ahead, this time knowing that this time there was at least a chance of it.

Robert was waiting at the chapel door, Judd beside him.

"We're sorry," Robert said, taking her hand.

"We should never have let it happen," echoed Judd, slipping his arm around her waist.

Meg leaned into him, squeezing Robert's hand tightly. "It's all forgiven – I'm getting a second chance, so of course I must offer you the same."

She stepped into the shelter of the chapel, spying Will waiting for her at the altar. Knowing that this time everything was right, she began the short walk towards him.

The End

ABOUT THE AUTHOR

Jennifer C. Wilson is a marine biologist by training, who developed an equal passion for history and historical fiction whilst stalking Mary, Queen of Scots on childhood holidays (she has since moved on to Richard III). Enrolling on an adult education workshop on her return to the north-east of England for work reignited her pastime of creative writing, and she has been filling notebooks ever since.

In 2014, Jennifer won the Story Tyne short story competition, and since then has been working on a number of projects, including co-hosting the award-winning North Tyneside Writers' Circle. Her Kindred Spirits novels are published by Crooked Cat Books, and her time-slip novella The Last Plantagenet? by Ocelot Press.

She lives in North Tyneside, and is very proud of her approximately 2-inch view of the North Sea.

You can find her online at:

Website:
https://jennifercwilsonwriter.wordpress.com/
Amazon:
https://www.amazon.co.uk/Jennifer-Wilson/e/B018UBP1ZO/
Facebook:
https://www.facebook.com/jennifercwilsonwriter/
Twitter:
https://twitter.com/inkjunkie1984
Instagram:
https://www.instagram.com/jennifercwilsonwriter/

OCELOT PRESS

Thank you for reading this Ocelot Press book. If you enjoyed it, we'd greatly appreciate it if you could take a moment to write a short review on the website where you bought the book, and/or on Goodreads, or recommend it to a friend. Sharing your thoughts helps other readers to choose good books and authors to keep writing.
You might like to try books by other Ocelot Press authors. We cover a range of genres, with a focus on historical fiction (including historical mystery and paranormal), romance and fantasy. To find out more, please don't hesitate to connect with us on:
Website: https://ocelotpress.wordpress.com/
Email: ocelotpress@gmail.com
Twitter: https://twitter.com/ocelotpress
Facebook: https://www.facebook.com/OcelotPress/

THE KINDRED SPIRITS SERIES

When the dead outnumber the living, the adventures really begin… Follow the 'lives' of the spirits inhabiting some of Britain's most famous sites, in the Kindred Spirits Series, available now.

A King, three Queens, a handful of nobles and a host of former courtiers…

In the Tower of London, the dead outnumber the living, with the likes of Tudor Queens Anne Boleyn and Katherine Howard rubbing shoulders with one man who has made his way back from his place of death at Bosworth Field to discover the truth about the disappearance of his famous nephews.

Amidst the chaos of daily life, with political and personal tensions running high, Richard III takes control, as each ghostly resident looks for their own peace in the former palace – where privacy was always a limited luxury.

With so many characters haunting the Tower of London, will they all find the calm they crave? But foremost – will the young Plantagenet Princes join them?

The bestselling Kindred Spirits series continues...

Along Edinburgh's historic Royal Mile, royalty and commoners – living and dead – mingle amongst the museums, cafés and former royal residences. From Castle Hill to Abbey Strand, there is far more going on than meets the eye, as ghosts of every era and background make their home along the Mile.

Returning to the city for her annual visit, Mary, Queen of Scots, is troubled by the lacklustre attitude of her father, King James V of Scotland, and decides to do something about it, with the aid of her spiritual companions. More troubling, though, is the arrival of a constant thorn in her side: her second husband, Lord Darnley.

Can Mary resolve both her own issues and those of her small, ghostly court?

On hallowed ground…

With over three thousand burials and memorials, including seventeen monarchs, life for the ghostly community of Westminster Abbey was never going to be a quiet one. Add in some fiery Tudor tempers, and several centuries-old feuds, and things can only go one way: chaotic.

Against the backdrop of England's most important church, though, it isn't all tempers and tantrums. Poets' Corner hosts poetry battles and writing workshops, and close friendships form across the ages.

With the arrival of Mary Queen of Scots, however, battle ensues. Will Queens Mary I and Elizabeth I ever find their common ground, and lasting peace?

The bestselling Kindred Spirits series continues within the ancient walls of Westminster Abbey.

In the ancient city of York, something sinister is stirring...

What do a highwayman, an infamous traitor, and two hardened soldiers have in common? Centuries of friendship, a duty to the town, and a sense of mischief – until they realise that someone is trying to bring chaos to their home.

Joining forces with local Vikings, the four friends keep an eye on the situation, but then, disaster strikes.

Can peace be restored both inside and out of the city walls?

THE LAST PLANTAGENET?

All Kate had wanted was a fun, relaxing day out, watching the knights jousting at Nottingham Castle. What she ended up with was something quite different.

Transported in a heartbeat from 2011 to 1485, how will Kate handle life at the Ricardian court? Even more importantly, how will she cope when she catches the eye of the king himself?

Find out in this 'giddily romantic' romp, set just prior to the Battle of Bosworth.

"A delightful novella" - Discovering Diamonds review, also shortlisted for Book of the Month, October 2018.?

Printed in Poland
by Amazon Fulfillment
Poland Sp. z o.o., Wrocław

49079807R00146